CASTLEBOUND

MAPLE
PUBLISHERS

CASTLEBOUND

Jess Whitaker

CASTLEBOUND

Author: Jess Whitaker

Copyright © Jess Whitaker (2025)

The right of Jess Whitaker to be identified as author of this work has been asserted by the author in accordance with section 77 and 78 of the Copyright, Designs and Patents Act 1988.

First Published in 2025

Text design ©Dinah Drazin
Chapter Header Art ©Canva

The author can be contacted at jess.whit@icloud.com

ISBN 978-1-83538-595-1 (Paperback)
      978-1-83538-596-8 (E-Book)

Published by:
  Maple Publishers
  Fairbourne Drive, Atterbury,
  Milton Keynes,
  MK10 9RG, UK
  www.maplepublishers.com

To Mum and Dad:
I did it.

BASIL

LATER

THERE'S A BANG. I'm in flight, yanked off my horse's back. Time speeds up. My body smashes into the ground. Gravel fires into my eyes like glass. A gash opens on my lip. My head batters against the cobbles. The thump, thump, thump of metal. A flurry of hooves. My neck, back and face all burn. The stirrup suspends my leg, jolting it in its socket. As my horse wrenches my hips apart, a scream rattles inside my head; it's mine. The castle is nothing more than a fading blur now, racing towards me as I die.

BEFORE

ARE YOU HAPPY, Basil?' Ragnar teased me as he clapped along to the lute. I looked up from the fraying buttons on my dress to raise an eyebrow at him. He knew I hated this song; did they have to play it at every wedding?

'No, I'm not. I despise this song, and you know it,' I shouted back over the hearty bellowing, giving him a playful thump on the arm.

He opened his mouth in mock offence. 'Hey, I was only playing!'

A small commotion across the tavern drew our attention. The bride let out a squeak as a gaggle of frantic women swarmed her dress to claim scraps of fabric from it. In a final attempt to escape, she launched her bouquet over her head. It landed with a clatter on the table next to Ragnar. The women flocked to it, allowing the bride to slip away unnoticed. But the eagerness dropped from their faces when they spotted the flowers in Ragnar's hands, a triumphant smile stretched across his face. Accepting defeat, the grumbling women slunk back to their partners.

He held out his prize to me. 'For you, my Lady Basilia.'

'Why thank you, Sir Ragnar! But, please, call me Bas.'

But before I could take it, he brought the bouquet to his nose and inhaled deeply.

'Mm, smell that, Bas!'

As I went to sniff the herbs, Ragnar pushed the bouquet into my face. I sighed at him. 'What am I going to do with you?'

He put down his drink and brushed the stray petals out of my eyebrows. 'You ought to figure that out soon, my angel.' Sloshing mead over his arm, he pointed at the newly-weds, 'That'll be us in a few moon movements.'

'Let's make that your last drink, shall we?'

'I'm not drunk!' Ragnar slurred.

I smiled, and he handed me the goblet.

Cheers erupted around us as the bride and groom shared a kiss. The dying screech of the horrid song faded away at last. Ragnar smirked at me.

'I bet you're only cheering because the song's over.'

'Oh, away with you!'

He pecked me on the cheek and drifted off into the crowd. A hush consumed the tavern as the bride took her new husband in her arms so that they could sway together—their first dance as a couple, surrounded by those who loved them. The bride, bless her, looked so happy like that. And to think, that would be me in a few—

A candle flickered out. Something was wrong. The groom had noticed it too. He'd stopped dancing and turned towards the door.

Footsteps. Hard and heavy. Outside.

Ragnar's grin slid off his face. The musicians stopped

playing, and the air thickened with a horrible anticipation.

Please don't let it be them. Not now. Not today. The tavern door flew open. Bated breaths became compressed screams as the dreaded armour came into view.

'We are here at the behest of King Vesuvius,' boomed one of the soldiers.

The chandeliers creaked ominously in the silence. I sent a quick prayer. *Please don't let the name be familiar.*

'Miss Antonella Endress, you are to come with us.'

My shoulders slumped with relief. Thank the Mother of Nature and the Father of Fate; I didn't know her that well.

But the relief was momentary before the chaos ensued again. The soldiers ploughed through the crowd, shoving those that couldn't scramble out of the way fast enough. There was a dull thud as the crowd parted, revealing Antonella in a heap on the floor. The soldiers grabbed the fainted girl roughly under the arms. It took two of them to drag her limp body across the grimy floor, through puddles of mead and out of the tavern. No one dared blink until long after the door slammed shut behind them.

When murmurs and movement finally returned to the tavern, Ragnar swooped over to join me.

'I just saw the bride crying in the back corner.'

'I'm not surprised. I swear, we can't have a single event without old King Vesuvius ruining everything. I thought he wanted to encourage marriages, not ruin them!' We paid our respects to the groom and went outside.

'Life would be so much better if he was gone,' Ragnar mused.

'Don't get any ideas, Ragnar, you'd die trying to kill him.' One of Ragnar's mates clapped him on the back as he passed. 'And everyone you'd ever known or loved would pay the price.'

'So he claims…' Ragnar mumbled.

I wanted the king dead as much as the next person, but Ragnar's friend was right. You'd be mad to try and commit treason of that level.

But what if you had nothing to lose?

Something pricked my skin and I jerked my clammy hand away from the guilty thorn. The flowers in the bouquet were already drooping, and the herbs had lost their scent. I let it drift to the floor, where it lay sadly for a moment, before being mashed up by a passing horse.

A soft mist caressed trinkets rolling on abandoned stalls. The king's soldiers had sent the bustling market-goers running in fear back to their homes overhanging the street—every window on the top floor of the half-timbered houses was bolted shut.

On the horizon, a flutter of crows dispersed from the surrounding forest canopy. Towering conifers brushed together in the chill, prickling the sky and providing solitude to the cluster of turrets in the centre. Not even the mountain range behind the woods could compete with the sheer stature of the castle, within whose stone walls sat the king of Yevonia, keeping constant vigilance over Magnate's Clearing, the village we called home.

A basket toppled from a nearby stand, throwing cooking apples across the cobbles. Ragnar stooped to pick them up, but they rolled from his grasp. Giving up, he looped his arm around my shoulder. I balled my fists, and we left for home in silence.

BEFORE

OHDEN WAVERED IN the door frame, his eyes red and puffy. He clutched a letter in his hand.

'He's killed her,' he said simply. 'She's gone.'

Bile threatened to rise in my throat. Ragnar guided me out of the way as his friend began to weep.

'Over a piece of bread!' he wailed, grabbing fistfuls of his golden curls and doubling over, his voice dripping with pain. My grazing horse startled and tried to bolt across the paddock.

'Shh…' Ragnar soothed, 'inside with you.' He led a snivelling Bohden into the house. I went to prepare a drink for the men. Something strong. Something that would ease Bohden's pain.

Vesuvius had erupted again, this time even closer to home. How much longer before he sent for one of us?

I pulled a bottle of wine from the pantry, unhooked a net of ginger and went back upstairs into the kitchen. I slammed two chalices down on the wooden table, poured the wine into them, chopped the ginger and stirred in the cloves while staring absent-mindedly at Ragnar's loom in the corner.

In the living room, Ragnar patted Bohden's shoulder as he sobbed over the death of his wife.

'The king'll use any excuse for an execution, but why, Father tell me, my lovely Matilda? I thought we came here to populate, not to die!'

Ragnar bit his lip. 'Well, the king can't live forever. One day all this will end.'

'I suppose you're right. I just hope it's soon.' Bohden gave a half-hearted laugh and dragged his nose across his surcoat sleeve. 'Thanks, Basilia.' He took the spiced wine from me and downed it. When he'd finished, he let out a sigh and wiped his mouth with the back of his hand.

'Thank you, dear.' Ragnar rested the chalice on his thigh and circled the rim with his finger, deep in contemplation.

I scooped up my wedding cloak, folded it and placed it out of wine-spilling reach. Not that it would have mattered anyway, as both the drink and the cloak shared the same deep shade of burgundy. After a little while of watching me smooth the fabric with unfocused eyes, Ragnar lifted his drink and stood.

'I am going to do it.'

'Do what, love?' I asked, not looking up from the cloak.

'I am going to put an end to all this pain and death. I'm going to kill that…' he fumbled for the right word, '…tyrant!'

I stopped smoothing the cloak.

Bohden chuckled uneasily. 'Don't be a bonehead, Ragnar!'

'I'm serious.'

I laughed nervously. 'Good one, darling, you almost

had me! Now, how about another drink—' Something was burning. 'Ragnar! Your stew!'

He slammed his wine down and rushed over to stir the contents of the crock. I sighed. The distraction couldn't have come at a better time.

'Do you want to stay for dinner, Bohden?' I asked.

'It's alright, thanks, Basil, I need to get back to my girls.' He groaned at the idea of telling them the devastating news.

'Of course. More for Ragnar!' I forced a laugh.

'Speak of the devil!' Bohden joked as Ragnar returned, flashing me a look as he sat down. I picked at my dress; this was not the last I would hear of his declaration.

Desperate to fill the silence, I took Bohden's letter from the table. 'May I read this?' I held it up.

'Why not?' he mumbled, anguish etched on his face. I unfolded the letter.

Bohden Bennett,

By the High Order of HM King Vesuvius, Matilda Bennett, your spouse, recently met her end at the gallows around quarter sun. The execution was decreed following her conviction for multiple counts of theft. As recounted by her executioner, her final mortal words to the Mother and Father were as follows: 'I am innocent! Please, my children!'

The Court of HM King Vesuvius.

BEFORE

THE AUTUMN RAIN drummed on the roof above our bed. Ragnar turned to face me, his body shielding me from the night seeping in through the broken window.

'Why do you hate the idea of the king being gone, Bas?'

Not this again. 'I don't. I hate the idea of you trying to do it and getting yourself killed. So you are not to do it.'

'Then who else? Think of all those families, dear. They deserve better, don't they?'

'Yes, but what if they…? What if you die? What if they kill me? It's suicide, Ragnar, both of us will die!'

'That's what he wants you to believe! It's all a lie to protect him from assassination! He won't touch me, Bas. The Father knows it's not my time yet. And I promise…' He took my hand and enveloped my fingers in his. 'I promise he won't lay a single one of his pruned fingers on you.' My fiancé's emerald eyes glinted with encouragement under his unruly eyebrows. The candle threw shadows across his face, hollowing it out. *He would protect me at all costs.*

'Can't you wait until after our wedding?'

'And how many people must suffer before then? Besides, it will be the most glorious wedding you have ever seen. Imagine it, my angel! You don't want a murder spree plaguing the happiest day of our lives, do you?'

'You can't do it alone!' I spluttered.

'Bohden will help me.'

'And if he dies?'

'He told me that if he, if he...' Ragnar squeaked, coughed and tried again. 'He told me that if he dies, no one will know to miss him.'

A milky tear trailed down his sculpted face. In the hazy candle flame, his skin took on a golden sheen. The Mother of Nature took her time carving him, making every inch perfect, from the moonlit contour of his muscles to the way his hand curved to fit perfectly in mine.

'But I will. I will miss him so much, Bas. However it will be a small sacrifice for all the lives we can save.'

I took a strand of his long, dark hair and watched the luscious lock loop around my finger, thinking. *Would I ever forgive myself if this beautiful man died?*

'So, may I, Bas? Do I have your permission to undertake this quest?'

I took a deep breath and stared into his emerald eyes. 'Swear that you won't die?'

'I swear on my life that I won't die.'

'Then you may.'

'Thank you, Bas. You won't regret this.' He pecked me on the cheek and blew out the candle. As expected, not long after the comforting sound of his obnoxious snoring vibrated off the walls, he pulled the furs right up to his nose and refused to give any up when I tried to tug them back.

Shivering a little in the draught, I followed him into a tormented sleep. Sleep filled with images of Ragnar's goodbye, Ragnar's back as he rode into the woods. Nervous anticipation—a dead weight. The possibility that I might never see his face again. Trees engulfed him with finger-like branches, stealing him from my grasp. Blood splattered from the king's body. He was dead. Angel wings burst from shoulder blades. The next nightmare came. Blood. Bodies. Ragnar's blood. His body. Puddles, no, rivers of blood flooded the castle, pooled, formed a cape. My wedding cloak. Me. Him. A wedding ceremony. I took his hands. But they were cold. I inspected his face. But it wasn't a face at all. Where his beautiful bright eyes once were, glassy black stones sunk into his face. We leant in to seal the marriage with a kiss, but his lips were cold and hard. No, wait, he had no lips; I was kissing his corpse.

I jolted awake, sticky with sweat. I must have yelped because Ragnar had awoken too.

'Bad dream?'

I turned over, sneaking back some of the fur. 'Yeah.'

'Do you want to talk about it?'

'I'm sure it's nothing.'

'Okay, my angel, if you're sure.'

I stared for a while at the water dripping from the ceiling. 'Why do you call me that?'

'What's that, Bas?'

'Your angel.'

He thought for a moment. 'Because when I look at

you, Bas, something tells me that everything's going to be alright. You're the best creation the Mother ever made.'

'No, love,' I murmured sleepily, 'that title goes to you.'

Smirking, he pulled me closer and his body heat soon eased me into a fresh sleep, void of nightmares.

RAGNAR

BEFORE

Heavy rain clouds sagged over the sleepy village as I strolled through it. Despite the warm orbs coming from the lamps either side, I had to force my eyes open; it had been a sleepless night.

I nodded a one-quarter sun greeting to an old friend trying to light the lantern on the face of his house. A cry of triumph escaped his scar-bisected lips as it flickered to life, completing the line of warm glows across the tightly packed houses. The flame drew out orangey-red undertones in his cheeks and ignited a spark in his garnet eyes. An intricate brooch holding his crimson cloak together twinkled in the lamplight. 'Good day, Ragnar!' he called back as I carried on down the street.

A black cat slinking across my path flicked its head towards me, lemon-yellow eyes wide and tail swishing. He broke into a run as a wagon full of glossy chestnuts buckled and dipped noisily over the cobbles. The young redhead dragging it huffed and puffed, her milk-white cheeks reddening with the effort.

A sparrow chirped a tune from a branch above me before taking off, dragging a clump of yellow leaves out of the tree with it. The bird flitted across the sky and landed in a small gap between a wall and a roof. I smiled a little as the bird hopped further into the gap, revealing a group of adolescent chicks. *The Mother's creation is stunning sometimes.*

I turned a corner and the scent of pork fat dripping hit my nostrils. My stomach growled. *Wasn't it strange how we Yevonians worshipped the Mother, yet reaped her ground for our own benefit?* I wasn't going to argue with it though; there was nothing I enjoyed more (besides making Bas happy) than a hot, hearty meal.

A tendril of smoke rose from the tavern's chimney, and I made a beeline for it.

A passing farmer wearing a feathered bycoket and lugging a sack I'd woven for him whistled a merry tune to himself.

'How's the harvest going, Luden?' I asked him.

'Not as good as last time, but not too bad thanks, Ragnar!' He gestured to the sack, brimming with barley. 'Enough to get through the winter. Have a good one!'

'You too.'

Outside the tavern, the weathered bartender was futilely sweeping leaves from the crumbling stone steps. 'Good luck with that!' I joked as another wave of leaves drifted from his feeble pile and danced down the path.

Adjusting the parchments tucked into my belt, I turned the corner and counted the houses on the left. Fifteen, sixteen, here it was: Number Seventeen. I hopped over makeshift dolls on the rounded step and rapped on the door three times.

'Who is it?' Bohden appeared at the window. 'Ah, Ragnar. Come in.' The door cracked open, and I slid inside.

The moment I'd crossed the threshold, Bohden slammed the door behind me. He raced around the house, bolting the windows and stuffing mouse holes with rags so that no sound could escape.

'Will your girls be out for long?'

'They've not long since left. One of their friends' mothers offered to take them blackberry- picking, so we have at least a full candle to plan before they get back. Walking helps them process their grief,' he added.

'Good.' Toddlers are known for being snitches. Having them in the house whilst we worked would be signing our own death warrant.

'I just don't know what to do, Ragnar. What did your father do when your mother die—'

'Ssh.' I cut him off. *We are not talking about that.* 'I'm sorry about Matilda. Come, light a candle.'

His hands shook as he tried igniting the wick. 'Here, let me.' With a whoosh a muted wash of colour consumed the room. Bohden glanced through the only window left ajar.

'All clear,' he informed me without shifting his gaze.

'You have the plans?'

'You bet.' I produced the parchment I had concealed underneath my beige tunic. Bohden helped me unroll my map over the table. 'So, we'll meet and enter the castle here.' I pointed with the tip of my dagger. 'Then we'll take out the guards stationed here, here and here,' I said, tracing the blade over the map.

I turned to my friend. 'When did you last sharpen your sword?'

He scratched his head. 'Last week.'

'Good.' I turned back to the map. 'Ah, you Father-forsaken thing!' I swore as the parchment rolled into itself. Bohden handed me two expensive goblets to hold it down. 'Right, now that's sorted…'

He hesitated, his hands twitching with nerves.

'What is it, Bonehead?'

'Ragnar, I don't know if we should do this.' He tugged at his honey-blond curls nervously. I stared into his large hazel eyes, and noticed a smattering of stubble had formed along his hardened jaw; fatherhood had claimed his kindred, fighter's spirit. He'd matured, and in doing so he'd become boring.

'But this is exactly what you need! What happened to the old Bohden? Don't you miss the good old days?'

Time to change tactics.

I turned my nose up at him. 'You're scared, aren't you, Bonehead?'

'What if I'm not the old Bohden anymore? We're not in a game now, Ragnar, this is real life. It's not that I'm scared for me, I'm scared for my girls. What will happen to them if I die?'

My friend shifted his weight from foot to foot. I held him with a cold stare. 'You remember the deal we made, don't you? At least give them a fighting chance.' My insides curdled at the cruelness of my coercion. I shunned the emotions; if I had any chance of giving Bas everything she deserved, I had to desensitise myself, even to my own friend's heartache.

'Why's it so important that we kill him anyway?' Bohden whined. 'He'll probably keel over in the next few moon movements anyway. We don't have to dirty our hands with royal blood.'

'Don't you want to avenge Matilda? Besides, sometimes, Bohden, you must get your hands dirty to unearth the biggest reward. Plus, if the old prune was to die of old age, his inheritance would just be wasted on another undeserving dictator and not someone deserving like me, you, the girls or Bas.'

Bohden scratched his head. 'What wouldn't you do for that woman,' he murmured.

'Anything, you Bonehead.' *He couldn't even begin to understand the extent of my love for her.* 'Because I have so much to give and she is the only one who deserves it.'

Exactly how far would I go for my fiancée's happiness? Well, regicide was a fairly good start. She'd love me unconditionally if I put a crown upon her silky hair. I would have died if someone gave all that to me in my old hometown.

BEFORE

I DARTED TOWARDS Bohden with my sticks. As predicted, he ducked out of the way. A triumphant smirk flickered on his lips as he raised his own weapon. How embarrassingly overconfident he was. I grabbed his arm, twisting it behind his back. His branch fell to the ground and I tapped my stick against his brassy curls.

'Bonehead!' I called, releasing his arm.

He dragged his hand through his wind-swept hair. 'Damn it, Ragnar!'

Barren branches scratched the murky sky as I wiped away the beads of sweat on my forehead. It felt good to fight Bohden, but winning was getting a bit boring.

'Ah, come on! That didn't hurt. You're only being mardy because I've won again.'

I opened my mouth to deliver the final blow.

'Don't…' Bohden warned.

'What are you going to do about it, you Bonehead?'

'Okay, you've done it now…' His arm shot out.

My nose exploded with white-hot pain. My eyes stung as I blinked back tears. I dabbed my upper lip with my fingers and smiled. At least my nose wasn't bleeding. 'You need to try harder than that to break it, Bohden.'

'I was just warming up.'

'Thief!' the baker's wife cried from outside a nearby shop a few metres away. My heart stuttered. She was pointing at Eric. He lived with our family and it was his turn to steal dinner. If she caught him, we would all be going to bed hungry that night. I chewed on my nails as we watched him cram the loaf down his tunic, and take off running.

The woman wrapped her thick cyan cloak around her. She glanced at her boots, trimmed with fox fur. There was no way she was going to get them dirty. 'You!' She thrust a finger towards me. 'Go after him!'

I smirked. 'With pleasure, Miss.' I bowed sarcastically and took after him. Eric tensed when he heard the approaching footsteps but relaxed once he saw it was me. His bare feet pounded the ground as he ran, his long legs eating up each stride. On any other day, I would have definitely beaten him in a race, but that bread meant the world to us.

Eric leapt over a bench. *Brace yourself, Ragnar.* My shins exploded with pain as I hit the bench and fell over it, landing face first into the mud. Eric threw a grateful smirk at me and disappeared round the back of the house.

I picked myself up, shrugging off the embarrassment. 'I'm so sorry, Miss, I would have caught him, but I tripped you see!'

The old bag growled her frustration and went back inside. A grin stretched across my face as I made for the nearby babbling stream.

'That was' – Bohden ran to catch up to me – 'dramatic.'

'I'd prefer the term "heroic", but thank you.' I splashed the icy water onto my face to dislodge the mud.

'Well, heroic Ragnar, you've still got mud on your nose.' He flicked it off. I thumped him on the arm in return.

'Ragnar!' my younger brother, Halvard, called from the house. 'Tea!'

I groaned. The thrill of the chase had quelled the aching hunger, but now it had made a reappearance.

'Coming!' I turned to Bohden. 'See you later, Bonehead.'

I ran up to Halvard, spooking the hens pecking at the ground. They scattered noisily across the makeshift pen. I leant over the woven twigs to soothe them. 'Sorry, Var.' I smoothed down the closest hen's ginger feathers. She clucked curiously at me. Halvard scooped up Father's armour and helmet from the drying stick to bring them inside. I ruffled his shock of ginger hair and stooped under the slanting doorway into the hut.

*　　*　　*

I squeezed past Eric's mother to my spot at the table. She was hanging a circular shield on the wall next to Father's quiver of arrows. 'There.' She admired her handiwork. 'Adds a pop of colour.'

'It looks nice, Mother,' Eric praised. Father grunted his approval. I rolled my eyes.

'Thank you, Eric,' she said, her radiant beam cracking

the face paint around her deep-set eyes. 'Good job with the bread.'

'He wouldn't have got it if it wasn't for me,' I muttered to myself, rubbing my sore shins.

The loaf puffed its chest proudly from the centre of the table. Waves of hunger swelled and crashed angrily in my stomach. The walls swayed. Icy rain drove into the house through the doorway. Water dripped from the sagging roof. I shivered.

Father's knife lingered in the air, poised to slice the bread into five even pieces. *Not nearly enough.* Halvard darted his green eyes up to me challengingly. Every time he did that, I caught a glimpse of Mother in him, like she was keeping us in check from the sky through my brother. But she'd understand that I needed the food more than he did. I needed my strength. Sure, Howard and Eric were both too weak to pass the initial test but there'd be plenty of food for them when I left for Yevonia.

I snatched the whole loaf and crammed it into my mouth. Father's knife stuck in the chopping board. The bread scraped down my eager throat and settled uncomfortably in my stomach. My mother's disappointed eyes bore into me from the above.

'Ragnar!' Halvard protested. Eric sucked in his hollow cheeks.

Father slammed his fist on the table, his nostrils flaring over his matted beard. 'You selfish boy!' he roared, spittle flying from his mouth. I thanked the Gods quietly that the knife was stuck in the board, and not still in his hand.

Eric's mother put her hand firmly on his arm. Her snowy hair whipped around her face as she shook her head.

Father growled. 'Halvard, Eric, outside.'

Hal shot me a look. 'He's going to kill you,' he mouthed, and they trotted off to a mate's house.

My brother was wrong. My fate was worse than death; it was a lecture.

'Listen, Ragnar, if you carry on like that, you'll kill your brother like you did your mother!'

Why must he bring Mother into this? Her abandoned blue yarn caught my eye from her old stool near the windowsill.

I put my face in my hands and wailed quietly. The bread crawled back up my throat, bathed in guilt. *Why do I always get so emotional every time he mentions Mother?* I rubbed the tears harshly from my eyes. *Get a grip, Ragnar.*

Father's hard stare faded. He sighed and dragged me into a crushing bear hug.

'Sorry, Ragnar. That was unfair of me to blame you. But what will it take for you to realise how serious this is? Listen, son, it's not enough for three growing boys, me and your mother—'

What would Bohden say if he walked past now? I wriggled free.

'That woman is not my mother,' I growled.

Father ignored me. 'Look, I get it. But if you marry someone in the New Land, you'll have to learn to put them first. Off you go.'

I trotted back outside. Father was right. Whilst I waited for Bohden to return, I swore to the Father of Fate that I would give my true love in the New Land the world.

BEFORE

'Psst, ragnar!' hissed Bohden, his widened eyes fixed on the muggy day outside.

'What is it?'

'The king's soldiers!'

'Where?'

'Outside!'

'Father's fate!' I scrambled for my dagger. Bohden dove onto the parchment and rolled it tightly. I snatched it and thrusted it under my tunic. The booming of the knights' boots rattled the house as Bohden and I ran around like headless chickens.

'Quick, out the back window!'

The footsteps grew louder and faster. I raced over to the window, my pendants and necklaces thumping against my chest. Bohden unbolted it. 'I'll see you at the castle in a few suns,' I told him, lifting one foot onto the ledge and quickly admiring my polishing work.

'May the Father be on our side,' Bohden prayed nervously.

I shoved my blade into my boot and checked it was secure. 'If there's one battle you should actually win, this is probably it, eh, Bonehead?' I leapt from the window. Birds took to the sky as I landed with a thud, straight into a pile of horse manure.

'Ah! My boots! I'd just cleaned them!' *What in the Father's name would Bas think I'd been doing?* My face grew brick-red with shame as I crept round the side of Bohden's house.

I froze. Bohden's stifled laughter had turned the knights' attention to me. 'Good day, sirs,' I mumbled, praying they wouldn't question me. Instead, they plugged their noses and hurried past me. *Pompous pustules.*

As I made my way home, the redhead's wagon, brimming with chestnuts, caught my eye. Bas's glossy, brown hair sprung to mind. I loved the way it cascaded around her shoulders when she let down her plait. I loved the way it framed her heart-shaped face. But as much as I loved her hair, it sent me insane every time she twirled mine around her finger.

I strode over. The woman (what was her name?) looked up and unfolded her arms. Delight flushed her face. From the look of it, business had been unproductive that day.

'Hello, Ragnar! Nice to see you out on such a fine morning!' She gestured at the overcast sky. It was not a fine day. 'Eh, well, not a fine morning, actually. Anyways, you look well!'

'Thanks, Helen.'

'Heather,' she corrected. Heather smiled and clasped her hands in front of her. Her gaze danced down to my boots. 'Erm, what happened?'

'Ah yeah, just a road accident. Listen, can I buy the

ripest, tastiest bag of chestnuts you have, please?'

'Certainly!' She swished an auburn braid over her shoulder. I watched her inspect each chestnut carefully before placing it in the bag. 'What's the occasion?' 'They're for my fiancée.'

Heather stopped. She was starting to get on my nerves; I had things to do. 'Is something wrong?'

A frown tugged at her thin lips. 'No, no. It's just… Your fiancée is a very lucky woman.'

'Yes, she is,' I agreed smugly. Basil is lucky to have me, but not as lucky as I am to have her. 'Can I have my chestnuts now, please?'

'Yes, of course.' She pulled the pouch's drawstrings tight. I handed her the money, took the bag, and turned to leave.

'See you around then, Ragnar.'

'Yeah, see you, Helen,' I said over my shoulder.

'*Heather*,' she whispered, but I was already on my way. *What a strange woman.*

*   *   *

I wiped my boots thoroughly on the grass of the paddock. Basil's horse put his head over the fence inquisitively. I stroked his forehead.

My muscles throbbed with fatigue and my ankles pulsed from the leap to the floor. I cringed at the lingering waft of manure emanating from my clothes.

Bas was at the kitchen window, preparing food. She

saw me approach and hurried to the door to greet me. 'Hello, love, how was it?' Her gorgeous, sapphire eyes lit up the sky when I presented her with the chestnuts. 'Oh, Ragnar!' Lightning crackled in my chest as I held her to me. If she got this excited about a bag of chestnuts, she'd go mad with adoration for me when I bought her the throne. *Father of Fate, what did I ever do to deserve this woman?*

My fiancée drew back. 'Look, Angus!' she said to her horse. 'They match your coat!' Basil took the bulging bag and pecked me on the cheek. 'Thank you, dear! Come on in.'

A swell of nausea washed over me. I clenched and unclenched my fists, hoping to undo the knots in my stomach. My journey to the castle was imminent, and I would be leaving Basil behind. *It's only temporary*, I told myself. *As soon as I've killed the king, we will be reunited. Besides, her best friend Florencia* (or Flossie, as Basil calls her) *will keep her company whilst I prepare the castle for her arrival.*

I put on a brave smile and went to undo my boots. On a second thought, I left them on; my dagger was still in there.

'Ah, Bas?'

She twirled to face me. 'Yes Ragnar?'

'Is it alright if I carry on…?' I tilted my head towards my parchments. I didn't say it aloud, for fear of the king's spies overhearing me.

She arched an eyebrow. 'Plotting?' she asked quietly.

'Yes.'

She sighed. 'Fine. Just don't stay up too late.'

My dearest Basil. If only you knew the surprise I had planned for you.

BASIL

BEFORE

INK DRIBBLED OVER the hand-drawn map abandoned beside Ragnar. I righted the bottle and dabbed
at the parchment, but it was no good; the ink had already
soaked through. I cursed quietly, and he woke with a
snuffle.

He looked up at me with sunken eyes. *He needs
a break.* I held out my hand questioningly. He placed
his hand in mine, and I whisked him off his chair. He'd
bitten his nails down to the skin, and his body creaked
and groaned in protest, but when he danced, he became
a bird in flight. Ragnar whirled me round, weaving,
swooping and sewing a rhythm between my two left feet.
But one clumsy step too far from me and we were both
lying in a heap on the floor, laughing like children. A
wisp of stress lifted into the air as we lay entwined. That's
the beauty of baltering; it's the Mother's way of letting us
release our troubles.

We were still laughing when there was a knock on the door. Blowing at the disruption, I heaved myself to my feet. My laughter evaporated when I saw who it was.

'We are here to take Ragnar Vernentide for trial,' droned a hollow-cheeked knight. Seasons of experience had left him void of emotion. Only Death herself had seen more slaughter than him. The stubby knight next to him was a blood-thirsty recruit. At Ragnar's horrified face, his tongue flicked to his lips. His piggy eyes darted around the room under his lowered visor and rested on the parchments. He strode into our house and snatched them up hungrily.

Ragnar pulled himself to his feet. His facial muscles were relaxed in a façade, but his chest strained against his tunic.

Get out of my house, I tried to say, but my voice snagged in my throat.

'Wh-what are you doing here?' I managed to splutter. The stubby knight handed Ragnar's work to his associate.

'This man is charged with plotting treason,' the tall one droned, almost bored as he flicked through the parchments.

'The most likely outcome of his trial will be execution,' the smaller one piped up.

They were going to kill him.

No. No. No. They couldn't.

The soldiers pressed their firm hands into Ragnar's shoulders. 'Get off him!' I demanded. The house whirled around us. We grew moons apart. I stretched out my arm to grab my fiancé, but the void pulled him back. Our fingers brushed, our names dancing in the air as we shouted for each other. Heartbeats between us, but also seasons. *I would never hold him again.* I was losing this battle, this tug of war between suns. If only I could stretch a little more…

The knights yanked him from my reach and manhandled him into a portable cell. I ran after them but, with a crack of reins, they took him deep into the woods. Ragnar was gone.

I closed my eyes. *This wasn't real.* Ragnar's pleading face stared back, etched into my eyelids. From then on, whenever I tried to rest, his cries tore into my head. He was everywhere and nowhere all at once and it ripped me apart.

NOW

STREAKS OF ORANGE lick the sky. Angus, my horse, plods down a side passage between the trees. Felled leaves ride the roots that stick out like veins under the forest floor. He disturbs them with every calculated step. We should reach the castle in one full rotation of the sun.

Shadows engulf us sooner than I would have liked. The sun dips below the horizon, dragging the last slithers of the flaming sky down with it. The darkness tosses the colours into a stormy ocean of ebony. Milky moonlight slithers down the cracks in the tree bark. Firs tower above us, closing us in, trapping us in our own thoughts. A chill carves down my spine as a gushing wind bangs them against each other. Knock. Knock. Knock. The sound all but drowns out the tuneful chorus of humming insects announcing the night. I hate this, I hate this, I hate this.

My shoulders slump and I let out a delighted gasp. Scattered lights blink back at me, illuminating the path with a balmy glow. Fireflies! I thought they were a myth! *Oh, Ragnar's grave, they're beautiful!*

They work magic in their dance, clearing the air around them in whirls and swishes. Confused, Angus tries to eat one. They soar, swoop and race between trees,

and then they are gone, plunging us back into the nightmare. The vice in my chest tightens.

Silence. A screeching, maddening silence.

BEFORE

I WAS SILENT the first time I read the letter, but my head was a screaming forest of thoughts.

Basilia Eldnic,
By the High Order of HM King Vesuvius,

I screwed it up, but I'd already seen the words swimming in my head.

Ragnar Vernentide, your partner, was beheaded—

What.

—at half-sun.

Ragnar. Dead.

The execution occurred four days after he and his accomplice, Bohden Bennett, were arrested for plotting high treason. Bohden Bennett received the same fate.

Traitor?

Master Vernetide's last words, as recounted by his executioner, were as follows: 'Tell Basil I'm sorry.'

This isn't happening.

The Court of HM King Vesuvius.

I broke in two. How could I have dreamt up something so horrible? Was it a dream? The letter screwed up on the floor told me not.

Bed. I'm overly tired. Forcing myself to breathe, I stumbled towards our bed. Yes. Surely, Ragnar would be there. Of course he would; he'd be tired out, bless him.

I imagined it all. Ha! Oh, how silly of me. I tiptoed to the bed so as not to wake him. The fur blanket rustled as I lifted it…

Ragnar wasn't there.

I threw up before I passed out.

NOW

Angus walks on cautiously. I wish he wouldn't. Sleep teases me, darting away every time Angus rustles the leaves underfoot. Pins and needles attack my legs as they thump against his flank. My other muscles quake with the effort of holding off the night, but I can already feel my thoughts spiralling. I could turn back. But then Ragnar's sacrifice would be wasted.

I'm so alone. If only the Mother knew what I'd give to have him with me. Perhaps if I die here, it'll be better. At least I'd see him again. All I have to do is to stop Angus and give in to sleep. *Oh, my dear Ragnar, I'm aching for you more than ever.* Icy breaths escape my chapped lips. I stretch my borrowed cloak tight around my body, but it does little to warm me. *I can't do this anymore, I can't take it anymore.*

A twig snaps. Angus flicks his head round nervously.

I pat his girth and whisper to him softly, but my own voice sounds detached. 'Can you remember our new trick Angus? Don't forget, when I say the command "Kiss", you press your nose to my cheek, okay?' I clear my throat. 'If you do it right, you can have some sugar. You can have lots of sugar and apples when this is all over.' He blows happily at this idea.

'You'll be able to brag to Domino about this adventure when we're done. Who do you think will win our next race with her?'

BEFORE THE LETTER

'R ACE YOU!' I called to Flossie as we reached the meadow. It was a summer's three-quarter sun, and dewy grass swished idly under the sleepy sky. A grin spread across her face, revealing dimples the Mother pressed into her cheeks. She stood in the stirrups and leant forwards over Domino's neck, her honeysuckle-scented blonde hair spilling in curls down her back. Tapping my horse's side rhythmically with my heels, I rose and pressed my chest to his muscular neck. The breeze dragged tears from my eyes. Angus gathered speed, the rhythm of his body fitting perfectly with mine. The pounding of hoofs rattled the air as we overtook the blur of Flossie and her piebald. Oh, what a feeling! Hoofs, one, two, three, four. One, two, three, four. I glanced back at the pair gliding over the lush swell of grassland. They were on our tail. We weren't going to let them overtake us. 'Faster, Angus, faster!' One, two, three, four. With one final push we crossed the tree that marked the finish line in first place.

Both of us heaved, bathing in our small victory. I relaxed in the seat and pulled the reins until Angus came to a stop. 'I win again!' I tormented Flossie whilst tugging on the bit. Angus veered into the pull towards the river.

Flossie came to a stop beside us, her spotty cheeks apple-red. 'I tell you, you're doing something right with that horse, sweetheart!'

'Well, what can I say?' I unhooked my feet and slid off my horse's back. 'Beatriz always says that he's bad luck' – I gestured at his four white socks – 'but I've never had a problem with him.' Angus opened his mouth, allowing his bridle to fall away towards the ground. I tried to snag it on my fingertips but missed. The noise rattled him, and he went to bolt. Thankfully, Domino's calm demeanour rubbed off and he settled. I picked up the bridle, a hot blush creeping onto my cheeks. Flossie smirked as she tucked Angus's stirrups up for me.

My horse leant over the freshwater gathered at the mouth of the forest. His lips flapped as he drank, distorting his reflection. Domino wandered over to join him. She nudged me out the way with her soft nose, snorting warm air onto my gloved hands. We finished untacking our horses and sauntered over the grass bank.

Flossie and I slumped down on the grass, and I let out a sigh.

'It's a shame the other girls couldn't come,' my best friend mused, picking at the daisies. I didn't mind. I preferred it when it was only us two and the horses.

'Yeah,' I nasalised.

The refreshed horses frolicked in the meadow. Dodging her flying legs, Angus nipped Domino on the dock. It was all fun and games, until Domino's hoof came dangerously close to the signature crescent marking branding his forehead. Angus dodged it expertly, but backed off anxiously. Sensing this, Domino turned to him, blew an apology and coaxed him back into their game.

'Oh Bas, I've had it up to here with the girl next door!' Flossie exclaimed. 'I get that she's just broken her wrist, but if she wasn't destroying the Mother of Nature's land, then it wouldn't have happened! She came round yesterday, sweet as honey and even asked for one of my apple pies!'

'After what happened last week?!'

'I know, right?' she scoffed, her snub nose crinkling. 'I love your dress, by the way, sweetheart. Purple really suits you!'

I blushed. 'Oh, thank you!'

We chattered until our muscles protested us sitting still for so long. Flossie helped me heave myself to my feet, and we kicked off our shoes and paddled in the river. The water lapped at our ankles, splashing our skirts' low hems, so we hoisted them up to our knees and waded further in. Flossie dashed the surface with her foot, sprinkling water over me. I opened my mouth in mock horror.

'Oh, you've done it now!' I gave her a playful shove. She lost her balance and fell into the water with a yelp.

She surfaced a moment later, spluttering and gasping. 'Curse you, Basil!' Water plastered her dress to her body and darkened her plaits. I cringed with regret, but she was laughing as she doused me in return.

Soon, the sun dipped below the meadow, casting a crimson glow into the sky. 'Red sky at night, shepherd's delight!' Flossie recited, wringing water from her pink overdress.

'Red sky in the morning, shepherd's warning!' I finished.

With our dresses soaked, it wasn't long before the breeze got to us, and we called the horses back. They were reluctant to stop rolling in the grass, but bounded over anyway. We tacked them up and mounted, sloshing half of the river down their body.

'Trot on, Angus!' I called. Angus began walking towards home, swishing his tail in Domino's face. 'Same time next week?' I asked Flossie as we reached the knobbly oak tree that marked our departing point.

'You know it!'

BEFORE

A MOON MOVEMENT after the letter, Flossie came round with an apple pie. She let herself in. A knock would send me into uncontrollable shaking. I would hide myself and will whoever it was to go away.

She placed the pie down on the table. 'You'll get over it one day.'

Shut up. Shut up. Shut up.

'No, I won't, he's the only person who'll ever make me happy, and he'll walk through that door any second.'

'Sweetheart, he's dead.'

How ignorant could someone be? 'No,' I snapped, 'he's not.'

NOW

SOMETHING SCREECHES. JUST an owl. Angus snorts. I keep talking. Angus relieves himself. I laugh. It's not funny, but I'm need an excuse to relax. If I don't, I'm done for. I sip my water. Is the forest lightening?

It is. The morning sky oozes with a deep shade of maroon. A bird tweets in a nest above. It's the most beautiful sound. Another bird joins in. And another, and another until the forest explodes with life.

I face the morning sky and laugh with relief. 'Thank you, Mother of Nature!' I cry. Finally, the longest night of my life has ended.

RAGNAR

BEFORE

I UNTANGLE THE crown from his matted hair. His blood taints the metal. I place it on my own head and the power surges through my body at once. I retrieve the dagger biting into his eyebrow and turn it in my hand. Taking my sweet time, I shove it back into my boot.

I've done it. I've killed him. The murderer's reign is over.

I turn to face my little crowd and slowly spread my arms out to the frozen guards. My power melts their stiffness, and they take a knee before their new king.

I've never felt so alive.

BASIL

BEFORE

Four of the girls are planning a get-together pic-
nic,' Flossie said, sitting herself on the edge of the
table near her pie. She was dangerously close to my wedding cloak. 'You should go, Basil. Might take your mind
off things. You know how the girls need someone to
keep them in check.'

I burnt holes in the floor with my eyes. Flossie shuf-
fled a little on the table.

'Can you remember when Domino used to kick out
and fart at the same time when she was excited?'

'Mm-hmm.' I stared harder.

How dare she? How could anyone be so self-ab-
sorbed? Her fingers crept closer to my cloak. I was rip-
ping at the seams, and all she could think to talk about
was her horse's stupid old habit?

'And we used to—' She touched my fabric. I exploded.

'Get out! I don't care about your damn horse or her

damn trick!' I flipped the apple pie off the table. It landed face down, crumbs of pastry strewn across the floor.

'Get out of my house, Florencia Rose.'

Her bottom lip trembling, she turned on her heel and whisked out of the room. I followed her out, but my sleeve snagged on the wall. *Last straw.* I screamed at it, and whipped my attention back to her. 'And may your husband be fated to burn as well!'

She wailed at the insult and left. I needed to hit something. Shaking with rage, I ran back into the kitchen and punched the wall.

'Get.' Punch. 'Out.' Punch. 'Get.' Punch. 'Out.'

Soon, my knuckles were bloody, and Flossie had abandoned me. It was so unfair. So, so unfair. 'WHY ME, WHY ME, WHY ME?' I screamed and screamed until my throat dried out and my tears gave up. I fell against the wall. The exposed stone scraped up my back as I slid down it and slumped on the floor.

I couldn't hold it off anymore. I stopped fighting and gave in to the numbness. Unfeeling. Unseeing.

How long was I there? How many candle marks? How much had the sun moved? How many moons even? My stomach mourned with hunger, and my head pounded from fatigue. But I stayed there. Dead to the world.

My black, dead eyes drifted over the mess on the floor aimlessly until they fixed upon something: my wedding cloak spilling off the table. I dived forwards and grabbed it, hugging it as if the smallest breath of wind would blow it away. I wanted to rip the fabric apart. I wanted to tear the world apart. But instead, I clung to it. It was the only thing keeping my broken body together and my soul from bubbling out of me.

NOW

THE BABBLING OF a stream catches Angus's attention. He tugs on the bit, and I let him lead us to it. We reach the water, and I dismount onto shaky legs. The fear the night brought has exhausted him, and he drinks deeply. Once he's satisfied, he dozes stood up. I don't have that luxury; I'm still exposed to the woods and any hope of sleep is long gone now. I stoop down and splash water on my face. My droopy eyes snap awake. Beads of sweat from my forehead flow into the water, taking the stress of the night with them. I refill my canteen and add crushed basil leaves to purify it.

The sun spills lazily through the shrunken trees. I take a seat on a coarse tree stump, so I can analyse the sky. We should reach the castle around three-quarter sun, but the early morning's redness suggests that harsh weather is coming.

My stomach growls. I take an apple from my pouch to munch on it. *What I'd give for a bite of one of Flossie's signature apple pies.* I'm craving the explosion of light, sugary pastry. Oh, and the perfectly balanced, gooey centre of tangy cooking apple!

Sour mush fills my mouth. I spit out the bad apple. My stomach growls again. Angus looks at me hungrily. I feed him the apple. I don't want it anyway.

Moments later, low, suffocating clouds plough over us, and the Mother begins to cry. Does she ever feel grief? When it rains, is that her looking at her creation and weeping at humanity's corruption?

Angus looks at me, eager to get going. He hates the rain. I tighten my boots and throw myself back onto his back, his dowsed hair already clumping together under the saddle. 'Move on, Angus.'

I don't need to ask twice. Thunder snarls in the distance, startling him. He rears a little but continues into the Mother's bellowing storm.

BEFORE

A FLASH OF lightning warped the shadows in the tavern whilst an angry fire crackled and spat in the pit.

'So, the messenger zipped round the corner, next thing I knew, the horses collide head on, and Juliana, Wren and Bronwyn are knocked off like skittles,' my friend Beatriz, the baker's wife, spilled to me. She twirled her long grey plait around her finger, darkening the tip with grease as she spoke. She hadn't even taken her dirty apron off in her haste to gossip, and there was a smudge of flour on her nose. 'One of 'em in the hedge, another in the road. As for the king's messenger… Basil, you should have seen it! So much blood! I must admit, I felt quite sick.'

'Are they okay?' I asked out of politeness. I didn't care if they were or not. I took a sip of my birch sap. 'Oh, for the Mother's sake!' I cursed as it spilt down my ashen dress. Yet another frock I'd ruined with my oafish hands. I wanted to go home.

A group of women huddled by the door, waiting for the storm to pass. On the table next to us, the village cobbler rested his face on his hand. With the other, he twirled his knife around his fingers with pure muscle memory to pass the time. Two untouched goblets of mead waited in front of him. As usual, his friend the carpenter was late for their weekly catch-up.

'The girls are fine,' Beatriz continued. 'Rushed 'em to the Wise Woman, bit battered and bruised, but they'll live. Impact killed the messenger though, poor man.'

I picked at my bandaged knuckles. It was the girls' own fault. *If I'd been there, I would have scolded them for sharing a horse in the first place.*

The rain roared at the window. A cry of delight rose from the next table—someone had won a bet. Ragnar used to bet with that group. My face ached as it forced back a sudden wave of fresh tears.

'Are you alright, Basil?' Beatriz let go of her plait and placed her hand on mine. 'Don't worry, it's okay! The messenger wouldn't have felt anything! Mother Nature's knuckles, I should've left out all the gore…'

The messenger didn't matter. He could burn in the hands of the Mother and Father for all I cared. Anyone that worked for the king could. Ragnar mattered. *Oh, Ragnar, you matter to me more than I can bear.*

'Anyway, how are the wedding plans going?' she asked naively.

Not great, given that my fiancé was dead.

I placed my horn of birch sap back clumsily in its stand and threw some money on the table, my tears blinding me. My friend's jaw was slack with horror; she'd completely forgotten about Ragnar's death. 'Thanks, Beatriz.' My voice hitched. 'I'm going now.' Ignoring her desperate apologies, I side-stepped out from between the bench and the trestle table, bruising my shins in the process. In my hurry for the exit, I bashed into Heather and her friends. 'I'm so sorry,' I whispered. She shot me a look that told me to 'burn at the Mother and Father's hands'. Wrestling back more tears, I flung open the tavern door. Icy wind slapped me across the face.

'Shut the door!' a large, brutish man in the corner hollered after me. I ignored him, put up my hands to shield my face from the battering rain, and ran for home.

NOW

IN THE WAKE of the storm, a coating of creamy mist has settled on the forest floor. Murkiness clogs the heavy air. We slow our pace to avoid a fall on the obscured roots. My fingers twitch at the reins. I want to scream. I ache to get there as fast as possible. I need to plunge my sword into the king's chest. Now.

Angus slips on a fallen tree. My heart falters, but he regains his balance. His nostrils flare as we ascend the hill. He's struggling. I stop him and dismount. I tip a little water from my flask into my cupped hand. His warm lips brush my palm as he drinks. I wipe away some of the sweat that has formed under his saddle. In the absence of hay, I offer him a graze, but he's more interested in the sachet of sugar swinging from my belt. He's been good, so I tap a small mound of it into my palm and close my sticky fingers around it. 'Angus, kiss.' I tap my cheek with my finger. He boops me on the side of the nose. 'So close!' I give him the sugar. We'll get it next time, I can sense it.

But every minute we spend doing tricks is another minute the king gets to live for. I pull myself back into the saddle and we walk on.

BASIL'S MOTHER

BEFORE

You miss your only daughter when she leaves for the New Land. Of course you do. You miss lots of trivial things like the fraying on her buttons from her picking at them nervously, the inaudible conversation she has with herself in her sleep and her fawn-like hair beneath your fingertips as you plait it.

It's easy to overlook the trivial things when you still have them; you can't overlook them when they are gone.

But you also miss a lot of important things: you won't see her fall in love. You'll miss her wedding, and her children if she chooses to have them. You won't see her grow into the independent woman you helped create.

'Last call for the females heading to the New Land!'

Sailors rolled bulging barrels onto a cargo ship beside the main transport vessel. Parents and siblings fought through the hundreds of gathered girls to return forgotten luggage and exchange last goodbyes. Sea salt rested on my tongue. Seagulls screamed overhead, and waves lapped at the disruption on the dock. The inky sea stretched for miles, rising and falling in choppy motions. Many of these girls unfortunate enough to pass the initial test would not survive the journey.

A blonde girl bounded over to us. 'Here, let me help you with that.' She took Basil's sack, lumpy with her belongings, and helped her lug it onto the gangway.

'Thank you! Are you going to the Clearing too?'

'Yes, I am!'

'Oh, nice! I'm Basil, what's your name?'

'My birth name is Florencia Aster, but it's a mouthful; my friends call me Flossie.'

Basil repeated the name under her breath to file it into her memory.

'What kind of man are you looking for in the New Land?' Florencia asked Basil.

'Oh, slender, nice hair, treats me right, you know? You?'

'As long as he doesn't have enough armpit hair to braid, I don't really mind.'

Basil's father let out a burst of laughter. I hit him angrily on the arm. As nice as she seemed, this blonde, bouncy teen had just waltzed into my daughter's life and pushed me, her mother, aside. I seethed at her as she hoisted her white dress and pink overcoat out of the puddles gathered between the rotting wood at her feet. She didn't deserve to watch my Basilia grow; I did.

There was a surge of people. Hard-hearted foot

soldiers herded straggling girls into the bottle-necked crowd trying to board the ship before it left. My heart ached, seeing girls of sixty-eight, seventy-two, seventy-six seasons old screaming and crying for their parents. But as reluctant as they were, the poor girls complied— going was better than execution.

Florencia took Basil's sleeve and they disappeared into the crowd.

I hadn't said goodbye.

I shoved into the chaos, ignoring the complaints that followed, but I was too late. I gawped as the gangplank was hoisted aboard. With a large sigh, the ship pulled out of the dock. With the two dark bodies gone, a lemony sun took its place at seven-eighths in the sky again. I could only wave my handkerchief at the groaning stern until Basil's transport vessel vanished over the horizon. I'd lost her forever.

There's one more thing I'll miss, and perhaps the most painful: I'll miss the death of the king who snatched my daughter away from me.

BASIL

NOW

WE CREST THE hill as the sun peaks in the sky. Underneath the ivory mist blanketing the valley bellow, the king will be dining on pheasant and decreeing another kill with a casual wave of his hand. There are probably soldiers knocking on the next wretched victim's door right now.

Two moon-illuminated silhouettes stood in the doorway. I screamed but my voice froze and shattered as soon as it reached the air. They grabbed him with spindly arms and set his head down over the kitchen table. One faceless, hooded figure curled his skeletal fingers tighter around the axe handle while the other hooded man pinned Ragnar down as he struggled. I forced all my energy through my eyes to stop the blade as it glinted in the air.

But my attempt was futile; the blade sliced through his neck like butter. Blood spewed over the floor, his limbs still twitching, his eyes still blinking up at me from his severed head…

I woke up. Not even sleep could hide me from the grasp of my mind.

A ball of blue yarn fell from Ragnar's abandoned loom and rolled across the floor, leaving a thread trailing behind it. Where was my fiancé?

My soul ripped from my chest, any lingering joy sucked out of it. I screamed into the void. A chill draughted in through the broken window. I touched my cheekbone, feeling the mark left by the sharp edge of the oak table. My legs fizzed from falling asleep on my stool. A stack of dirty dishes toppled over the table, and crumbs of bread interlaced in my knotted hair. My linen dress was damp with sweat. I rubbed at my eye, feeling it move in its socket. I didn't want to be awake either.

Two ladies rode past the window on horseback. One of them donned a veil; she'd recently got married, lucky thing. I caught a snatch of their conversation as they passed: 'Did you hear that there've been four new executions?'

The recently married woman gasped. 'How tragic!' she cried dramatically.

What day was it?

I groaned; Flossie wasn't due round for a few days yet. Combing my hair, scrubbing my nails, changing my clothes and feeding me properly was her job. And it was all done in silence to avoid another argument. Until then, I had to scrape along on my own.

Outside, a thick, grey snow smothered the greenery of the paddock. It fell so hard some nights I thought the sky was falling. The Mother was testing that winter. She pelted me with dark, sunless ages and long, icy nights. On the days Flossie dragged me to my bed, without Ragnar there to block out the chill in our chamber, I nearly brushed with Death herself a few times. Dying would have been a welcome refuge, for now only a dull flicker kept me going. But as the snow frosted the forest around the house, I was certain I would never feel the soothing caress of a spring day on my face again.

Slumped against my pillow, all I could do was surrender to the all-too-familiar endless slog of crashing, drowning waves. Every movement of the sun was the same cruel torment of numbness, nightmares, numbness, nightmares. That wasn't living. It was barely existing.

NOW

Aᴺᴰ ᴘɪᴇʀᴄɪɴɢ ᴛʜʀᴏᴜɢʜ the mist, the twisting turrets loom, ominous and clawing Motherward. The blur of my grief screams at me. Cast into a break in the woods below lay the vast castle gardens. Arched stairways spiral around the towers, all meeting at the entrance. From the grand doors, a cobblestone path cuts down the centre of the flowerbeds to join up with the one that Angus and I are on.

This place houses a murderer. A murderer who causes endless suffering in the settlement that he created. This place is where Ragnar took his last breath—where the king will also take his. My blood races with determination; I'll need every ounce of it to push us into a free era.

BEFORE

I T'S HER PARTNER,' Flossie explained, smoothing her powder-blue dress underneath her and perching on a broken stool. Bottles of various alchemy lined the shelfs behind her. She craned her neck to look at the labels. 'The king executed him a while back. I've done what I can, but I thought I'd bring her here.'

I nodded solemnly, fiddling with my buttons. The village Wise Woman pottered over to me and placed a hand on my head. She pulled my eyelids up and peered into my eyes. I wanted to move my head away, but she handled me carefully, as if I was something fragile. The last time I'd felt hands as motherly as hers was when Flossie cleaned a gash Angus had accidently caused over my cheekbone. The Wise Woman circled me, tapping me here, tapping me there, lifting my arms. I let her do it to me, feeling like a doll in the hands of a loving child.

She pointed at my scarring knuckles. 'Get some honey on those.' Flossie had already told me to do that. I wasn't going to. They didn't hurt anymore. Nothing did.

I followed Flossie's gaze up to the ceiling. Bodily fluids stained the interior roof. Her age must have restricted her to only cleaning the walls, for they were spotless. What I would give for me and Ragnar to grow that old together, but now we'll never—

'Basil.' Flossie's voice snapped me back to the present.

'Hm?'

'Your remedy.' The Wise Woman extended a piece of parchment out to me. I squinted, trying to make out the old lady's scrawl.

'What does it say?'

'One cup of lemon balm tea at half sun until symptoms ease,' Flossie read out, taking the parchment.

'Very popular, so it's hard to get at the minute. I'm all out in my stocks, I'm afraid,' the Wise Woman chimed in.

'I'll see if I've got some. Thank you.' Flossie helped me to my feet.

'Thanks,' I muttered. A lot of help that was.

The sunlight burned my eyes. Around us, snowdrops burst from the ground. A warm breeze ruffled my mint-green dress around my ankles. The Mother was releasing her icy grasp on the Clearing at last.

A couple strolled past us, the woman holding a tiny baby in a bundle of furs. Flossie cooed at it.

'How's he sleeping, Letitia?'

'Brilliantly, thanks, Flossie!' Letitia bragged, looking soppily at her baby. 'You're a lifesaver! Although Kian here was wondering…'

I squeezed my eyes shut. Why couldn't that have been me? Desperate to shut it out, I buried my head in my friend's chest. Thankfully, Flossie took the hint, wrapped up the conversation quickly and took me home.

RAGNAR

NOW

MY HEELS CLICK on the gilded floor as I pace in front of my throne. It's been ages since I sent that letter. I whisk on my heel to face an attendant, catching a glimpse of panic in his eyes at my sudden movement.

'Summon Mrs Florencia Rose. Tell her the king wants to see her, and if she does not comply, I will use force.' Perhaps losing her best friend will finally convince Basil to come after me.

BASIL

NOW

I SET ANGUS into a fast trot downhill. But it's not fast enough. Branches whip at my face as I stand in the stirrups. 'Faster, Angus, faster!' He snorts his disapproval but breaks into a canter, his hooves pounding rhythmically against the ground. The trees thin out and disappear behind us. I lean forward in the saddle, fixing my eyes on the cobblestone path running up to the mouth of the castle. The wind knots my hair, floods my eyes, roars in my ears. My fern-green travelling cloak billows and screams behind me, the Mother filling my heart with her approval.

The burning in Angus's legs claws its way into my chest, natural and fierce. But no matter how hard he tries, he can't gather enough speed to quell the roar of adrenaline in my gut. A tinge of blood dances on my lips. The blurry memory of Ragnar's faded face flashes in my mind. Soon the sweet taste of revenge will extinguish the flames of rage. His sacrifice will not be in vain.

BEFORE

FOUR SEASONS HAD passed since the letter came pronouncing Ragnar dead. There had been forty-eight deaths in that time.

I wove my clean hair into a plait, and picked up the clothes on the floor.

Ragnar was dead.

Finally, it had sunk in.

My love. My fiancé. Gone.

But it was okay.

For the first time since Ragnar's death, I was okay.

FLOSSIE

BEFORE

'DID YOU FEED Angus as well?' I asked my husband Cider as he came back into the house.

'As if I'd forget!' He kicked off his boots. 'He's been making a right fuss without Basil to look after him. Domino's only just keeping him together.'

My eyebrows knitted together. 'Poor thing.' I picked up a comb from my bedside table and sat on the floor. I dragged the teeth through my thick mass of frizzy blonde hair, running my fingers through it simultaneously. *Mother of Nature, please bless poor Basil with a speedy recovery.* Not even being able to look after her own horse is breaking her.

'How's your shoulder today?'

'Still sore.'

'Mother bless you, sweetheart. Domino is such a pest!'

Cider shrugs. 'Well, at least I got my foot out of the stirrup before I fell, so no harm done. I'm just getting old!'

'You're only ninety-two seasons!'

Cider chuckled. 'Well done helping that boy earlier by the way,' he praised, hanging his cloak up on the door and adjusting the horseshoe nailed to the wall above it. 'He'd really messed up his leg!'

''Twas nothing a bit of honey and a bandage couldn't fix.' I smiled. That was the first thing my father ever taught me about first aid; some honey and a bandage for a cut works wonders. My heart throbbed. I missed him so much.

Cider placed a hand on my shoulder and squatted to look me in the eyes. 'Flo, I think it's time you started putting yourself first a bit more.'

'Cider!' I gasped. 'You know how much Basil is struggling at the moment! Sweetie, I love you dearly, but please don't say silly things like that.'

The freckles mapping his face disappeared into a crease forming between his eyebrows. 'That woman's becoming too reliant on you. Sometimes, Flo, we have to do seemingly selfish things to help our friends more in the long run.' A strand of his mahogany hair fell from his bun. He blew it out of his eyes, not breaking his stare.

I turned my head and separated my own hair into three sections. Behind me, my husband jutted his jaw in frustration. Irritation settled deep in my chest. Why was he trying to make me selfish?

A sharp knock sliced through the tension. 'That's the second time this week…' Cider strode over to the window.

'It's a messenger.' The colour drained from his face. My

heart stopped. *Please, Mother of Nature, help me.* The king had already sent one messenger demanding that I meet him at the castle. He'd told me that if I declined, they would give me one more chance and then use force.

'Stay here, please, sweetheart.'

'Flo, what's going on?'

I surged up onto my toes to squeeze his shoulder. 'Nothing you need to worry about.' The lie was bitter on my tongue. Swallowing became impossible as I opened the door.

The messenger wasted no time. 'Miss Florencia Rose, the king requires your presence.'

'Tell the king that I will never go to him after what he's done to us.'

The young man hesitated. 'Miss, are you sure—'

'That's Mrs to you. And yes, I'm sure. I'm not a child.' My mouth tingled. 'Now, please leave my house.' I was about to crack, so I slammed the door in his face. Once his footsteps disappeared, I rested my head on it, breathing heavily. That was a horrible thing for me to do; he was only doing his job.

I avoided Cider's harsh brown eyes and went back to plaiting my hair.

BASIL

NOW

WE SWITCH FROM a canter to a gallop and glide down the hill; I'm nearly there.

Oh, why didn't I embrace this in those long days after Ragnar's death? I spread my arms, letting the sun's rays beat down on my chest and warm my heart. Running with Angus is the freedom I needed so deeply back then, the thing that would have put the Mother's spark back into my heart. My horse's back becomes fluidly smooth as he runs. I close my eyes, soaring, living, feeling. In any other circumstances, life wouldn't get better than this.

Soon this will all be over and Flossie and I can race across the meadow again. I open my eyes. The lazy seven- eighths sun floods the gardens, the only shadows drawn from the castle. I'm ready. I place my hands on my sword's hilt to check it's still there.

If only Bohden hadn't turned Ragnar in. None of this would have happened. It's a good thing Vesuvius executed Bohden or I would have killed him myself.

Wait a minute. Bohden had two kids with his wife not long after their marriage. Why would he risk his life, if he was the only parent to left to look after them?

Unless he had no choice… BANG.

BEFORE

BANG. BANG. MY lungs strained against my ribcage as the awful panic crept in. Ragnar's face floated behind my eyelids, pleading for help as the knights dragged him away…

My vision evaporated as Flossie opened the door.

'Basil?'

'The one and only.'

'You're here.'

'Yep.'

'At my house.'

'Oh, for the Mother's sake, Flossie, get to the point, will you?' I teased. Honestly, Flossie was the loveliest friend, but she could be so dumb sometimes.

'You're here!' She flung her arms around me, squeezed me tight and held me at arm's length to look at me. 'You're in the outside!'

'Yes, I am.' I giggled. It was good to be out.

'And look at your shoes! Are they Ragnar's breeches? You're going on a long journey, aren't you?'

'Ssh, Flossie!' She mustn't give the game away before it's even begun.

'Okay, that doesn't matter. What matters is you've got colour in your cheeks and, and—'

'Flossie!'

'Your hair is neat and—'

'Flossie!' I yelled.

She dropped my plait. 'Sorry.'

'I need a few favours.'

'Of course, Basil, anything, but I need to tell you something first—'

'Just save it a minute, Flossie,' I told her, returning a greeting to Cider, her husband, who had appeared at the door. He leaned against the door frame and drummed his fingers along his folded arms.

'Trying out a new style there, Basil?' He gestured at my grey tailored cloth leggings and dark handmade tunic, accented with intricate golden lace. A leather pouch swung from my belt, holding an apple, a purse of sugar, a flask and purifying herbs. Everything else I needed for a night and a day was in a sack tied to my saddle. The whole outfit was from Ragnar's chest. His second-favourite pair of boots squeezed my feet, but at least it would keep my blood from pooling on the long journey.

'Oh, no. I'm going for a ride in the woods, and riding skirts are so uncomfortable! Speaking of which, could I borrow your travelling cloak? And a sword, please?'

Cider was known across Magnate's Clearing for his 'Rose Blades'. Every man in the village owned one of his excellently crafted tools. They were used to carry out everyday tasks such as cutting up meat and hacking away branches. He'd even made Ragnar's beloved daggers, which had gone missing after my fiancé's execution.

Cider's pouty lips drooped. 'Erm, what for exactly?'

'Cider, hush, sweetie. Let the girl have a little fun, her fiancé is dead after all.' Flossie gave me a knowing side-eye. Relief surged through me. She'd figured out what I wanted to do and knew to keep it a secret. If spies overheard us, my demise would come before I could finish my task.

'I may have a spare you can borrow.'

'Excellent, thank you!' He stooped under the doorway and disappeared into the house.

'So, where are you heading, Basil?' Flossie asked casually.

'I'm castlebound.'

Flossie raised an eyebrow. 'You just made that word up.'

'No, I didn't. It means I'm heading towards the castle.'

Flossie shrugged. 'Fair enough.' She lowered her voice and I leaned in to hear her. 'Just to clarify, what's all this for?'

'I'm finishing what Ragnar started.'

'Sweetheart,' she sighed, 'I really don't think you should. You see—'

'Flossie, this time it will be different. I've nothing left to lose. I'll be fine.'

'Well, Basil, about that...'

She had the best intentions, but I didn't want to argue. 'Flossie, please, I know what I'm doing. Now, where's Angus?'

A smile crept onto her face. She spun on her heel and

went round to the back of the house to fetch my beloved horse. I kicked at the gravel until she returned, leading Angus. He neighed in delight when he saw me.

'It's good to see you too!' I grinned as he shoved his nose into my palm. I stroked the crescent on his forehead with my thumb and patted his nicely-filled-out barrel. Flossie had plaited his tail and even fashioned him a bow from a scrap of green ribbon.

She beamed. 'Nice to see you pair reunited,' my friend trilled, handing me a pouch.

'What's this for?'

'It's a first-aid kit. You never know when you might need one.'

I stuffed it in my travelling sack. 'Thanks, Flossie.'

Cider returned holding a scabbard resting upon his fern green travelling cloak. A glassy, black hilt protruded from the top. He passed the onyx-handled sword to me. It was light and comfortable in my hand, the icy spiral design on the hilt flowing deliciously under my fingertip. I withdrew it smoothly, marvelling as the blade gleamed in the sun. Angus jolted a little. The weapon was glorious; I couldn't wait to delve it into the king's heart.

'You be careful with that!' Cider shouted over his shoulder as he slunk back inside.

Flossie raised an eyebrow at Cider as I attached the holster to Ragnar's trousers. 'I'll try!' I joked, sliding the sword into place. I thrust my arms into the cloak and went off to prepare Angus for the long journey.

THAT NIGHT

PHLEGM JUNKED UP the back of my throat as we set off from the house. Flossie clung to Cider's arm as they wished me luck. I pulled the pouch's drawstring tight and clipped the brass buckle shut. Satisfied that it was secure, I let it fall to my hip. Finally, I adjusted my sword holster to stop it tapping against Angus's hip.

It hit me that I could die doing this. Was I ready for death? *Well, I had nothing to lose.* And at least I would be with my darling Ragnar again, plus the Mother and Father.

A moment later, Angus and I stood at the threshold of the forest, debating the best way to get to the castle. The main passage, or a longer side passage? The side passage would be arduous, and the main path would be too risky. We'd likely run into one of the king's messengers, and if they caught us, we'd be history.

NOW

F OR THE SPLIT second after the bang, the air chokes with silence. My heart slows in my chest. Time drags to fit its pace. It must have been a pair of castle doors slamming further ahead. *Nothing to worry about.* I go to place my hands back on the reins, but I'm too late.

FLOSSIE

BEFORE

THE TREES SWALLOW Basil up. She'd gone, off on her quest to kill King Vesuvius.

Father's fate! I didn't tell her! Basil is off to kill a king that wants me dead! I had to let her know. I at least needed to say goodbye. If the king doesn't kill me, he'll kill her. I turned to Cider, 'I didn't tell her!'

'What's that?'

'I was going to say goodbye! Sweetie, they're coming for me! They're going to kill me! You need to tell her…'

'Who's coming for… Flo, look out!'

Rough hands grabbed my arms and pinned them behind my back. My heart dropped to my stomach. I squirmed and lashed out, but I couldn't wiggle free. I threw my head back, hoping to hit my capturer, but he twisted my arm in retaliation.

A slim-faced woman took out a scroll. 'By order of His Majesty the King,' she read, looking down her nose at me, 'Florencia Rose, you are under arrest for refusing to comply with authority.'

I refused to let them take me away. I kicked at the knight's shins. My foot exploded with pain as it struck his greave. 'Hold still you filthy bitch!' he thundered in my ear, mead lacing his stale breath.

I hate that Mother-deprecating insult. 'Get off me!' I pummelled the soldier's armour, and his grip loosened slightly. Cider wasted no time. He grabbed my arm and pulled me into his chest.

'Cider, tell Basil—'

'Forget her, Flo!' Terror twisted his strong features. 'What's happening?'

Grimy fingernails scraped across my cheekbone, sending me to the ground. Cider roared in pain and crumpled behind me. What had she done to him? Was he okay? Lightning shot up my arm. I shrieked. One knight twisted my arm horribly behind my back, whilst another tied my hands together with a fraying piece of rope. 'Take her to the carriage.' I dug my heels in. Two other men appeared from nowhere to pitch in. I lost my footing and fell.

'Cider!' I tried to call, but mud filled my mouth. I spluttered and choked as they shoved me into a bare carriage. Two grey draught horses pawed the ground, uncomfortable in their facial armour as the foot soldiers forced them to walk. I craned my neck to see my husband stirring on the floor. *Thank you, Mother of Nature,* I thought to myself as I rocked in the carriage. I didn't dare speak as the horses worked their powerful shoulders to drag me further and further away from both my concussed husband and my doomed best friend.

Maybe Basil saw the soldiers approach and was heading back to check on me. No, how would she know? She'd taken the side path.

BASIL

NOW

I'M IN FLIGHT, yanked off Angus's back. Time speeds up. My body smashes into the ground. Gravel fires into my eyes like glass. A gash opens on my lip. My head batters against the cobbles. The thump, thump, thump of metal. A flurry of hooves. My neck, back and face burn. The stirrup suspends my leg, jolting it in its socket. As my horse wrenches my hips apart, a scream rattles inside my head; it's mine. The castle is just a fading blur now, racing towards me as I die.

I have no time to panic. An oncoming stupor smothers the sensation of my body being torn to pieces. I must get free. There's only one thing for it: I wrestle my sword out of the holster as my vision closes in.

There's a slash as it jams into flesh, followed by a scream. I throw myself out of the way, crunching my bones. The rush of legs stops.

Thud! A wheezing Angus falls to the ground.

I rise to a stoop and nurse my face, my vision seeping back. My horse's eyes are wide with terror. I crawl over to him.

'Get up, Angus.' He doesn't.

'Please, Angus, you have to.'

He snorts softly, but he doesn't move. 'Angus, get up!' I roar at him. My pulse drums angrily in my head. I straighten up, but the gardens spin around me. I bend over, pressing my hands into my eyes until the sickening whirling stops.

My leg screams in protest as I push at his hefty body. This must work. He needs to get up. I heave through sobs, but despite my arduous attempt to move him, he still lies there. A pool of blood starts to spread underneath us.

What did Flossie say you should do with an open wound? 'With any cut, always apply pressure to stop the bleeding first,' I repeat. I scramble for my pouch, but there's a huge rip in it. Her first-aid kit is nowhere to be seen. I curse and place both hands around the sword. I push on the gash but there's too much blood. It just keeps gushing and gushing, seeping through my useless fingers.

It's raining again. The droplets splash into my swollen eyes and roll down my cheeks. They land on his coat and wash the sweat away.

'Angus, please.' I give up so I can hold his heaving body. 'Angus, I'm so, so sorry.'

They're the last words he hears before his rattling chest stops moving. He's gone.

*   *   *

This is not happening. This cannot be happening. I can't bear it. I can't breathe. There must be something, anything I can do to save him. His warm lips will never touch my cheek in return for sugar. I will never escape my grief again. He can't die. My anger, my hurt, all those lost seasons rip from my mouth in a scream that is primal and raw.

A strip of silver sticks out of the brown blob I'm resting my head on. The sword I once thought was so alluring. It's Angus's blood on my sword, Angus's blood smeared on my hands, on my clothes, Angus who I've killed. I despise myself for this. I want to tear myself apart for this. I hope I'm burnt in the hands of the Mother and Father after this. Even that is better than my new reality. I want to kill someone for this.

My mind is detaching from my body, plunging me into a dream-like state. A fog settles between my mind and reality, easing the impossible pain.

The king. My body curses him from the bottom of my lungs. I need to kill him, like he killed Angus. And Ragnar. Bohden's wife. All of them. But not just them. Me. The fall of that blade snatched my life from under me too. Only the Mother and Father have the right to send Death upon their creation. But right now, I have a duty of fate. I'll make the king suffer for this. I'll make him beg for the mercy of Death. And, because I have a duty, I'll smile sweetly and give it to him, in the slowest way possible.

I find a jagged rock and pocket it. But a stone won't protect me from the guards at the entrance. As much as I'm putting it off, I need the sword.

I close my fingers around the bloody hilt and try to ease the blade out. It squelches on the way from his body, splurging blood into my face. The blood's hot and sticky, crawling over my skin. I throw myself away from him onto all fours and retch, but my stomach's empty. I wipe the blood off with the shreds of my sleeve. Squeezing my eyes shut, I wrench the hilt again until finally it comes free with a sickening crunch.

I force myself to study Angus's face before I become too numb to remember. I splutter at his beauty, despite the speckles of blood contaminating the white crescent on his forehead. I gently close his eyelids, his skin still warm and tender beneath my fingertips, but they spring back open. I remove his bridle from over his ears and take the bit from his mouth. I detach the bit from the bridle, wipe the blood on my cloak and attach it to Ragnar's belt. As soon as I've done the Father's work, I'll give him a proper send-off. I plant a kiss on his forehead, avoiding his dead stare, and and leave him covered with my travelling cloak.

NOW

Now that the fogginess has gone, it's like someone has crushed my leg with a brick. It takes an
age to reach the three-tiered fountain in the centre of
the castle gardens. My mouth is drier than soil in the
middle of summer. I go for my water flask, forgetting
that my pouch and sack both burst open when Angus
dragged me across the cobbles. All my things have fallen
out. No matter, I have other priorities at the minute.

I abandon the sack, kneel over the rim of the fountain
and thrust my puffy face underneath the cool flow of
water. Everything aches. My neck is stiff and my fingers
tingle, but I thank the Mother's ground that is the only
head injury I sustained. Neighbours of mine have had
falls like that and died.

As for my leg, the tender skin embellishes a mustard
yellow colour through a rip in Ragnar's breeches. I test
my foot on the ground gingerly and wince. I scan the
area for a stick. The only one I can find is tangled in a
rose bush. Pricking my fingers on the thorns, I wiggle it
free, and use it to bear my weight. It'll have to do for now.

Conical conifers line the path, providing a refresh-
ing pop of life to the gardens. The flowers that bloom in
spring shrink back and wither as I limp past, and bushes

that have snatched the forest's patchwork leaves snake around the walls. The turrets bundle together like sticks, defensive and menacing. Ivy claws up the new masonry. The sheer scale of the architecture drops my jaw. Candles flicker behind the grated windows above the entrance, giving life to the terrifying beast.

NOW

THE CASTLE'S STONY eyes stare me down. This is it. Here, at last. The birthplace of my sorrow and the deathplace of my lover. Not averting my gaze, I spit on the step to the grand entrance before stepping up onto it.

I take the cold metal ring in my clammy hand and slam the knocker against the wood twice. Whilst I wait, I grind the heel of Ragnar's boot into the stone, to hurt it, to crush it.

The massive doors creak open. Is that blood tainting the air, or metal? Sending a quick prayer for the latter, I limp straight into Death's gaping mouth.

NOW

CARVED MARBLE PILLARS, flecked with gold leaf, hold a murky ceiling. My gaze follows the floral designs that snake up the walls, joining at the top of endless passageways. Locked blades and armour accent the entrance hall, striking warm light into my sore eyes. Such a beautiful slaughterhouse.

An immense tapestry stretches across the back wall, depicting little, stitched people on boats. Girls on one, boys on another. Little yellow details circle the clearing, making it glow, as the people set foot on it for the first time. A large crown floats overhead, symbolising unity. Every person is frozen, beaming up at it. Above, the title reads, 'Yevonia'.

What a load of shit! People were miserable when they stepped off the boats, seasick and homesick. They only thing we dared to look forwards to was a forced relationship. My relationship was genuine; I was one of the lucky ones.

Vesuvius tore us from our homes, our families, everything we'd ever loved. We had to start over and build up a society, a group of strangers armed only with false hope. The only ounce of experience that comes with age we had was from the singular Wise Woman that came over with us.

We are filtered out and killed if we aren't 'perfect'. We're forced into relationships. Our children will be nothing but weapons, tools for the king and his heirs to use at their disposal. Future generations will know this depiction as fact. They'll remember the massacre of the Yevonians as a victory, and they'll hail King Vesuvius for it.

The Father of Fate would never let that happen.

The doors bang shut behind me. I shudder; that was the noise that caused Angus to spook. Tearing my eyes from the tapestry, I scan for my next move. Engraved into one of the archways are the words, 'Throne Room'. That's the one I need.

The two men who heaved open the gate approach me. One of them I recognise as the knight who dragged Ragnar to his death. He holds himself upright, flouncing his authority. 'Purpose of visit, Ma'am?'

I've not thought this through. *Oh well, I'll improvise.* 'To damn the king,' I mumble to myself, before forcing my anger through my fist up into his jaw.

The guard falls to the floor, unconscious. Who knew watching all the fights in my childhood town would ever come in handy?

My knuckles are already yellowing from the metal in the helmet's strap, but there's no time to soothe them. I only have a few moments until he stirs. The other knight closes in. The room stutters around me. He grips his sword menacingly, flexing his bulging muscles under his armour. The crest of his helmet swishes as flicks his head round to the passageways. *What do I do?*

He calls out for help but my elbow to his gut cuts him off. He gapes like a fish out of water and falls back. The heavy boots of backup guards echo through the entrance hall. I slip behind a displayed suit of armour. They pour into the room from multiple branches. It's a Mother-made miracle they can't hear my heart threatening to spew from my chest. Soldiers stride past my hiding place. My breath stagnates in my lungs. There's a call for a 'Medic!' as I dip into a nearby passage, adrenaline tickling my stomach.

The dying sunlight beams in through the identical open arches on either side of the Gothic hallway. I make for the candlelight illuminating the end of the passageway. Portraits of royal generations long gone mock me as I limp past. There's the occasional shrine made of cheap metal, but not the gold and jewels our Creators deserve. So Vesuvius thinks himself above the Mother and Father? If only I could ignore the taunting pain in my leg; I want to stick my stone in his head as fast as possible.

Thirty strides away from the end, pain forces me to stop at a large tapestry depicting the king's coronation. Once the throbbing in my bruised ribs has dulled, I admire the art on the wall. I reach a hand up and stroke the stitches of the king's weathered features, tracing his droopy eyes with my finger. I curtsey before it, withdraw my sword and rip it down through the king's face. I smear the other side of my sword across his woven palms, so he will burn at the hands of the Mother and Father stained with Angus's blood. Satisfied with my artwork, I whisk on my good heel to carry out my fantasy.

RAGNAR

NOW

A MESSENGER RACES forwards and bows hastily, eyes fixed on the floor.

'She's here, Your Majesty.'

A smile stretches across my face. At last. 'Good. Tell the guards to let her pass.'

'She's already got past, Your Majesty.'

I smirk. She was always a clever thing.

BASIL

NOW

I**T'S NOT HARD** to find the throne room; the door boasts ornate engravings that loop and swirl back on themselves. Four guards stand sharply on either side. A dozing doorman opens his eyes. 'What?' he grunts.

'I request to speak to the king.'

'I can't let that happen, I'm afraid, sunshine.' The rickety door attendant heaves himself onto his exhausted legs. I ground myself with a steadying breath and reveal my sword. The soldiers brace.

The doorman scoffs, 'You think I ain't seen one of them before?'

With one hand I reach for the sword. I adjust my grip on my stick with the other. I flash my blade. The guards draw their weapons. All eyes are on my hilt. I extract my sword and delve it into the ground. Leaning on it, I swing my stick around and it locks with all four of the guard's advancing hands. Their weapons clatter to the floor as they clutch their bruised knuckles. White hot pain flicks up my face. I dab a finger on my cheek. It's wet with blood.

Oh, the doorman! He's got a sword! I sweep the stick behind his knees, and he falls over. My destroyed ankle pulsates with my sudden weight on it, but my focus is on the sword flying into the air. I try to catch it but miss. My palm screams as the blade slices across it. Clenching my teeth against the icy pain, I run my blade across the guards' arms as they crouch to retrieve their swords. They writhe in agony over their wounds. So much for 'Protectors of the Throne'. It's incredible that no one else has assassinated the king yet.

The doorman's sword only lightly grazed my cheek, but my hand is another matter. It's bleeding, a lot. I take Ragnar's tunic in my sliced hand and squeeze it to suppress the bleeding. Agony shoots up my arm. I breathe through each wave of exhausted nausea that threatens to overwhelm me.

Eventually, the storm calms to discomfort, and I move towards the door. The stricken door attendant mumbles something, and I stop to listen.

'I wouldn't kill him if I were you.'

I pause. 'But you aren't me.'

The doorman groans and places his head down in defeat. In a final attempt to restrain me, a guard grabs my injured ankle. I shriek as pain curls up my leg, and stab at him with my stick until he shrinks away. I take a shaky breath, perhaps to quell the pain, perhaps to prepare myself, and push open the door to the throne room.

RAGNAR

NOW

I'M ADJUSTING MY jewels as the door flies open.
And my stunning, bloodstained little angel hobbles in.

BASIL

NOW

RAGNAR SMILES AT me.

'Hello, Bas.'

Oh, Mother of Nature. The corpse still has a voice in its throat.

*   *   *

Is that truly him? How is it possible? Why's he alive? I should be happy. I should be running into his open arms. But I don't. Because he's dead.

'How?' I force out to the bejewelled man sat back on the throne.

'Father's fate, Bas, I thought you would at least be happy to see me.' It's so good to hear his voice instead of the king's that I'm torn between kissing him and stabbing him.

But has madness claimed him? 'Happy? Happy?! Ragnar,' his name tastes sour from disuse, 'how can you expect me to be happy? Have you ever woken up and not wanted to be awake? Yet when you go to sleep there's no rest there either? Have you ever trudged through the mud of grief in the dim hope for better days? And when the end finally flickers on the horizon, a mere breath will extinguish it? I blocked everything out. It was torture, Ragnar! You put me through all that torment and now you have the nerve to sit there, alive and grinning?'

His grin droops slightly under his broken nose.

'Is Vesuvius behind this?'

'No, no.' He chuckles softly. 'I suppose I owe you an explanation.'

That's the least he owes me. I tilt my chin up, signalling for him to continue.

'After Vesuvius executed Matilda, I knew I had to do something. The poor Yevonians deserve so much better...' He looks at my sword warily. I slide it into its scabbard but keep my hand rested around the hilt.

'The only way to get close enough to the king was to get arrested. So, I got Bohden to turn us both in.' Oh yes. There's something not lining up about Bohden.

'And what of him? Where is he now? He was a single father to two young children; he wouldn't go on your suicide mission with so much at stake.'

Ragnar shuffles a little on the throne. His hooded eyes dart around the room, refusing to meet mine. Clouds smother the sun outside, darkening the grand room. The candles lining the walls waver in their torches.

'Ragnar. Is he alive?'

'No. He was stabbed by a guard.'

There's still something he's not telling me. I soften my tone. 'But he didn't go willingly, did he? Ragnar, why did he agree to go with you?'

'He did go willingly.'

'Don't insult my intelligence, Ragnar Vernentide! I've known you long enough to tell if you're lying; you crease your brow!'

'Fine.' He relaxes his brow, and the line between his slashing eyebrows disappears. He sighs. 'I told him that if he didn't agree to help, I'd kill his family. Happy now?'

I had no words.

'I'm sure you'll understand. Don't worry about his girls, their friend's mother has taken them in. Besides, Bohden was a minor sacrifice.'

Had he really said that? What monster had he become?

'Hold on a minute—you sent your childhood best friend to death, and you're telling me this as if you're commenting on the weather? What is wrong with you?'

'People change, Bas.' The shell of my lover stares at me. His once-loving green eyes resemble only hollow caverns, the left circled by purple bruising.

'But you know what won't change, Ragnar?' My cheeks burn, the cut threatening to bleed again again. My vision swims. 'The scars you gave me. The pain you've caused me. Tell me, why did you fake your death? This better be the best explanation I have ever heard, or I'm going home.'

RAGNAR

NOW

S HE MUSTN'T LEAVE. Not after all this.

'I think leaving would be a mistake, Bas.'

'The only mistake I ever made was loving you.'

She knows that's not true. 'It was the only way to get through to you.'

'What, by taking my heart and mashing it into a pulp?'

Ouch. 'Bas, how else could I ensure you would join me at the castle?'

'Not in the sickest way possible! You could've let me in on your plan?'

I smile at her innocence. 'My dear, we both know that would not have worked. I needed to guarantee you would come here without announcing it to the whole of our Clearing. I knew your undying love for me would force you into revenge-seeking. But, as far as the village is aware, the king is alive, and I am dead. If it was ever to get out that I murdered the king, my days would

117

be numbered; there are still some idiots out there who agreed with his regime. I would be assassinated before the crown could touch a single hair on my head.'

Hurt smacks across her pretty face. I don't like it.

'Why didn't you send a private messenger?' she whispers, her brimming tears catching the candlelight.

I sit up. 'I did.'

'As if you did! I received nothing of the sort.'

What? 'The letter, remember?'

'The only message I ever got about you was your death notice!'

'I sent a messenger to you after I killed the king!'

Something clicks in her mind. 'The accident.'

'What accident?'

'When was the message sent?'

'About six moon movements ago. But why does it matter?' I tap my foot impatiently against the golden floor. She ignores me. 'Basilia!' I erupt. 'Answer me!' Her diamond eyes flash. Regret washes over me. Why did I shout at her? She's been through a lot already.

'Your messenger died in a horse accident before he could get the letter to me.'

I sit back down, satisfied. 'How sad, I liked him.'

*　*　*

'So if the king was dead, who sent forty-eight others to be executed? I sincerely hope that they're not actually dead.'

My stomach plummets. I hadn't thought of secretly keeping them alive. Ah well, too late now. 'Well, you knew the king. If four seasons had passed without any executions, people would become suspicious.' I loathe myself for doing it, but keeping my survival a secret was the only way to get Bas here so I can give her everything she deserves. And it worked because my angel is standing in front of me now. I snatch another look at her. She's zoned out. 'Basil?'

'Mm?' She's miles away, but her mouth responds obediently.

'Bas, did you hear me? Are you alright?'

'Yeah,' she says vaguely. 'This feels like a dream.'

For once in my life, I don't know what to do.

BASIL

NOW

THE FOGGINESS IS back. I'm detached, almost like a part of my consciousness has shut down. I can't process what Ragnar has said. He is stood in front of me, concerned. Forty-eight deaths. I thump Angus's bit against my leg. Forty-nine. 'You killed Angus as well.'

Finally, that mask cracks. The skin between his chin and bottom lip creases. It's subtle, but I've got through to him now. 'How did—'

I tell him how it all happened. I tell him how Angus dragged me down the path, how, in those moments, I brushed against Death herself. How I drove my sword into his chest to save myself. I tell him how Angus fell beside me, bleeding out. I tell him how I held my horse as he died. The king I set out to kill is dead. *Angus's death was pointless.* Ragnar rubs the back of his neck and looks away. He knew how much I loved Angus.

But then he realises that he's no longer on his precious throne and instead on the same level as an enraged woman with a sword. He runs backwards up the stairs and sits, never taking his eyes off me.

'From the sound of it, Bas, you killed him.'

The room stutters around my eyes again. My knees weaken. Torment riddles his face at making such a crushing claim. He suppresses it and continues.

'Since you hadn't arrived yet, I summoned Florencia. She was to send you here. And if you didn't comply, you would most definitely follow her to the castle.'

'Flossie never told me anything.'

'That doesn't matter. You're here now. The past is out of our hands. All that matters is what happens next. Listen carefully, Bas; you will announce that the king died of old age and left you as his heir. You will rule, and I will guide you from my 'grave'. Together, we will serve justice to Yevonia.'

RAGNAR

NOW

S HE STARES AT me in disbelief. I drink up her gorgeous eyes; *how I've missed them.* She blinks. 'You're a cruel man and you will drown in your own carnage.'

I gasp quietly. Surely, she can see that the small sacrifice of those people was vital for her happiness? 'I only want what is best for the people,' I protest calmly.

'You're a liar.' She glares at me, catching me off guard again. Maybe I don't understand her as well as I thought.

'How so?'

'You don't want justice for those people.' She unsheathes her sword for extra effect. 'You don't want what's best for the Clearing. No, you crave power. You want jewels and banquets and Death at your fingertips. You want everyone to bow at your feet. And what better place to rule than a village, a village that he populated just so tyrants like you have an excuse to live out their daydreams? Because that's all this is. This, this village is full of pawns in the late king's sick, killing game, people to fuel his lust for blood, his Father- forsaken fantasy of—'

I grin. 'Your intelligence never fails to amaze me,' I praise, but she still needs me to nudge her in the right direction. *This is why I'm perfect for her.* 'But can't you see? I do want all this, but I want all this for *you*. I want *you* to have jewels and banquets and Death at your fingertips. I want everyone to bow at *our* feet.'

She furrows her brow. 'But, Ragnar, why do you think I want all this?'

'Basil.' I wish she could see herself the way I do. 'My angel, since I first laid my eyes upon you at the dock, all I wanted in this world was to make you happy. And now, as king, I can finally do that. Yes, it's unfortunate that Vesuvius used us as deer in his hunt, but the beauty of that is you can change it! When you choose to become queen, you can do anything you want.'

She thinks about this. 'Anything?'

I nod. I've got her now. 'So, Bas, will you rule beside me as the public face of justice?'

She bites her pearly bottom lip. 'I will never ever rule alongside you, after what you made me do. If a mere throne will diminish your morals, I don't want anything to do with you.'

I grit my teeth. Fury tenses my muscles. I didn't expect her to be so rebellious. She's acting almost… ungrateful.

'Don't you understand? Bas, I tried to ease you into it, but you did all this yourself! Ignoring your friend, not coming to the castle sooner, killing your horse, oh boohoo!' *Too far, too far, too far.* 'No matter, my angel, I'll forgive you. You just need a little convincing.'

I gesture to a nearby attendant, whose ropy hair hangs limply around his face. 'Bring her in.' The attendant nods and leaves the room.

Why doesn't Basil want to be Queen? When I was younger, I would have killed for this power, and I'm handing it to her on a plate.

The attendant returns, followed by two white-knuckled knights, each gripping a chain, a third tailing with a whip. I wince as Bas slackens her jaw, her doe-eyes following them as they lead my greatest weapon into the room. Bound and gagged between them is Basil's dearest, wide-eyed friend: Florencia.

FLOSSIE

NOW

'NOW, BAS, ANSWER me again,' Ragnar growls. Basil snaps her attention back to him. 'Will you rule beside me?'

Don't agree to it, sweetheart, please. You don't know what you're getting into, and this can only end badly. A sweaty gag traps my voice, so I shake my head at her frantically. My shackles rattle with the motion, drawing the king's eye to me. The soldiers give the shackles a sharp yank.

'Never,' she growls finally. I let my heavy shoulders slump.

Lightning shoots up my spine. The pain is impossible. My back is on fire. Through the black spots consuming my vision, Basil looks at me helplessly. I squeeze my eyes shut, focusing on my breathing.

Abies alba buds, more commonly known as silver fir, are harvested for their infection-preventing qualities, I recite from my father's books to calm my pounding heart. *They are found in mountain forests, at around one thousand to sixteen thousand strides above sea level…*

My ears are still ringing when the king asks, 'Will you rule beside me, Basil?' The chains rattle as I shake my head again—the icy metal bites into me as the soldiers tug again, firmly. Sweat and fear throng the cool air.

'No,' Basil decides finally, her bottom lip trembling. This must be so hard for her, but she's doing so well.

Another detached crack. A moment of tranquillity and then fire. Boiling water. My back splits open, an active volcano, spewing heat, the force of the sun compressed into a single lash. Unable to take the burden of the pain, I fall to my knees. My back screams for relief. I'll do anything to make it stop.

'Come on now, Basil, don't make me do this to you.' Ragnar's disturbed face is almost desperate.

Aloe barbadensis, more commonly known as aloe vera, is harvested for its soothing properties…

My streaming eyes move sluggishly to Basil's fingers. They stroke a piece of metal attached to her belt. Angus's bit? Where's Angus then?

'Come on, Basil, look what you're doing to your poor friend! If you agree, I'll make it stop. You're not the kind of woman to let this continue, are you? So, will you rule beside me?'

I long for an end. I'd rather die than have Basil agree to this. *Aloe vera is a plant species of the genus Aloe, and is mainly found—*

Basil's answer to Ragnar's last prompt dices my thought. The word echoes in my ears, crystal clear as it drags through my brain: 'Yes,' she says quietly.

No sweetie. No, no, no.

BASIL

NOW

FLOSSIE GROANS. THE knight lowers his whip. Ragnar swats his hand. 'Take her away. The coronation will be in two days.'

His crooked lips twist into an empty smile. It's been four seasons since I last saw him, and his face had become a blurry memory, but his glowing smile always stuck in my mind. This man's smile is void of his usual glow. Ragnar is void of his usual glow.

Flossie's clinking chains become distorted, as if I'm underwater. My vision greys, dulling around the edges. Ragnar melts into a blob of darkness in front of me. 'Ragnar.' My voice is warbled. My knees give out and everything stops.

RAGNAR

NOW

Basil dips, and her eyes gloss over. *Her sword!* I race down the steps and ease the blade from her soft grasp. Steadying her fragile body with my other hand, I place the weapon on the floor and slide it out of the way. Her knees buckle. I grab her as she crumples, forcing the hand that had held the sword into her chest. An attendant moves to help, but I wave them away. They might injure her further.

In this awkward position of me cradling her head, I lower my sweet angel to the floor to relieve my arms. 'If she doesn't wake in several candle marks, fetch a medic,' I announce to no one, suppressing the terror that threatens to shine through my voice. 'And if she dies, every one of you in this room is for the axe,' I add, slamming the door behind me.

BASIL

NOW

Did i faint? Why am I lying on the floor? I was stood up, and now I'm not. I find myself surrounded by a crowd of people, suffocatingly close. I try to get to my feet, but a plump attendant eases me back down. 'Get up slowly, Miss.' Too many people talk at once. Why didn't I bang my head?

The crowd eases off, relieved. And the courtiers kneel before me. It's pointless, given that I'm lying on the hard floor and they are still above me, but I don't think they know the proper etiquette for addressing a fainted royal.

I'm going to be queen. The blood rushes from my head again. I need to speak to whoever got me into this mess. 'Where's Ragnar?' The staff exchange confused glances. 'The king,' I clarify with a small shudder.

'The king has left, Miss.'

The king. King Ragnar. I stare at the ceiling for a while, trying to take everything in. But I can't. I'll never cram all that into my mind, let alone the sheer number of people he's…

An attendant stifles a cough. I must look ridiculous, lying on the floor whilst they wait for me to say something. But I have no words for them. So much for a good first impression.

'Leave me be, please.' I need some space. 'I'll be fine.'

'As you wish.'

The moment the grand doors slam behind them, thoughts drown me.

The last time I fainted, Ragnar was dead. This time, he's alive. Or is he? His body still moves, his heart still beats, his lungs still fill with air, but Ragnar's not alive. Not the Ragnar that I once knew and loved. Not the man who wove magic when he danced and made the sun brighter with his smile. Not the man I rode through a forest at night to avenge, the man who made the best stew for me when I was sick, my love, my world; that Ragnar died a long time ago.

NOW

Are you ready, Ma'am?'

Nope. 'I suppose so.'

And my coronation begins.

An elder drops a bulky cloak on my shoulders. The vice in my chest tightens. There's a collective scrape of chairs as the court rises in the Great Hall. The doors burst open, exposing me to the waiting crowd. I was so overcome with shock when I first saw this room that I barely acknowledged it. Now, I have to resist gawking at the sight before me.

The entire spectrum of colours surges through the stained-glass shrine to the Mother and Father, echoing the size of the room. A waterfall of gold-threaded deep red fabric flows from it, down the back wall before ending behind the thrones. A carpet of the same shade runs up the length of the floor, stopping just short of the throne where Ragnar sits expectantly.

My jaw drops. Every part of the room has been carefully designed to accentuate the king as the centrepiece, and it's done to perfection. Not a single part of the heavy fabric that buries him is visible under all the jewels. A garnet-studded chain hangs from his neck, weighed down by a large sapphire in the centre.

His jewels catch the light from the windows on either side, sparkling like the surface of a river, temporarily blinding me.

A scribe scribbles studiously, his quill scratching through the smothering heat. Someone coughs.

Come on, Basil, they're all looking. Put one foot in front of the other. My dress, a deep shade of regal violet, ripples around my legs as I walk down the endless aisle, the crushed velvet sticking to my sweaty back.

My vision swims in the light. How embarrassing would it be if I fainted now? I speed up my pace. The women bearing my cloak behind me clack their heels frantically, trying to keep in time with my heavy limp. One lady clips my heel, and my shoe comes loose. She whispers excessive apologies into my ear, but I dismiss them with a sigh. This is not going well.

Oh, what I would give for Flossie to be here now. This would have gone a lot smoother if she hadn't been locked in her chamber.

After an eternity, my party reaches the steps to the thrones. I lower myself wonkily onto my haunches before the arc of elders. The cloak bearers place the cloak down behind me and my shoulders slump with the weight of it. I try to adjust my shoe subtly with my foot. *Damn it!* I've kicked it further away.

The head elder takes a pot from his fellows, dips his fingers in it, makes a religious gesture with his hands and says a quick prayer to the Mother and Father. Slipping my shoe back on just in time, I rise and scale the gilded steps, careful not to stub my toe on the crust of rubies that line the edges. Am I doing this right? *I hope so.* When I reach the new throne assembled beside Ragnar, I whirl on my good heel to face the courtiers. My long sleeves echo proudly as I stretch my arms out. Tiny golden stitches flow over my chest and split off at my knees to line the base. I do love this dress, but I hate the situation.

The autumn air is thick with anticipation. The stoic people watch me from the immaculate rows of chairs under the arches. There are so many eyes boring into my forehead, scanning my face for the tiniest glimpse of panic. Somebody thrusts a staff into my clammy hands and backs down the stairs. I long to press the cold metal against my sweaty forehead. Plaited loops of hair tickle the back of my neck, still reeling from the momentum of the walk.

There's a crown on Ragnar's head. I shut my eyes. *Breathe in, breathe out.* I pick at the gold stitches cuffing my sleeves. I hate this.

It's my turn. I open my eyes as the head elder raises a circlet and lowers it onto my head. The sharp edges dig into my hair, but at least it cools my forehead.

I perch myself on the bony throne, watching the head elder lead a court of bows. We've prearranged not to shout Ragnar's name in the chant to avoid anyone overhearing us.

'All hail Queen Basilia Eldnic of Yevonia, and may the Mother of Nature and the Father of Fate bless her!' the head elder bellows. My new title sends a shiver up my spine.

'Long live the queen!' The crowd hollers back. Ragnar looks over in my direction.

'Long live the queen!'

He has a huge grin plastered on his face.

'Long live the queen!'

He nods at me and turns to face the crowd again, waving royally as they erupt into false cheers. I don't want this. I don't like it. I need to stop him before this goes too far. But our escorts usher us to our rooms before we can share another word.

*   *   *

The remedy trickles into the bowl as the medic wrings out the cloth. She lays it on my lower back, the liquid dripping down my sides and splattering on the floor. A stinging pain sears across the torn-up skin. I ball my fist and bite down on it, hard. She wrings out a second cloth. I yelp this time, but again, the discomfort is brief.

Ragnar takes my hand in his. I squeeze it reluctantly. 'I know, I know,' he murmurs as the medic works. *No, you don't know.*

Suddenly I'm galloping through a clearing.

A bang curses through my head and the image flips upside down.

The flurry of Angus's mane turns to a whip, cracking down over Flossie's back. Her muffled scream.

I'm galloping through a clearing.

A bang curses through my head and the image flips upside down.

The flurry of his mane turns to a whip, cracking down over Flossie's back. Her muffled scream.

I'm galloping through a clearing.

A bang curses through my head and the image flips upside down.

'Bas?' someone drones.

'Yeah?'

The flurry of his mane turns to a whip…

'Are you alright? You've gone quite pale.'

I must have rolled off the bed, because now I'm stood at eye level with Ragnar. He puts his hand on my shoulder. I suck in air to calm myself. I'm fine. I force my feet into the ground and clench my fists until the memories float away.

I open my eyes. Ragnar is screaming at the medic. 'Harm my queen again, and I'll break every bone in every body of everyone you've ever known!' She startles and spills the remedy. A knot the size of Yevonia forms in my throat. 'No, Ragnar, it wasn't her fault.'

His nostrils flare. 'Get out,' he tells her. 'I hope you burn at the hands of the Mother and the Father.'

She runs out, leaving the remedy spilling onto the floor. He sighs and picks it up. A tear trickles down my cheek. *What's wrong with me?* The bed sags as Ragnar sits beside me. He wipes the tear away with his thumb.

'Ragnar, you have to let Flossie go!'

'Bas.' He cups my face in his hands. I bat them away,

but he persists. 'I can't do that. She knows that I'm alive!'

'At least let her see her husband!'

'No.'

'Ragnar, I don't want this! Let her live her life!' I stare out over the woods. The tears are back, tickling my eyes, threatening to overflow. 'Let me live my life.' I hate him for what he's done to her. I want more than anything for him to let her go, to ease her pain a little. But how can I hate a man that loves me so much?

He stands up and looks at the wall, clenching his jaw. 'This is your life now.'

'I can't have that, Ragnar. Please, let her go.'

'Over my dead body!' he snarls. His face softens.'What do you want instead? I'll give you anything, but I can't free Flossie yet. How about a painting? A dress? A nice brooch maybe?'

'Nothing, thanks.' He can always get me those things if I change my mind.

'Come on then.' He puts his arm around my shoulders to guide me. 'Dry your eyes, my love, we have a country to rule.'

NOW

A MESSENGER STEPS towards us, his head bowed respectfully.

'Speak,' Ragnar commands.

'The country is in a mourning period for the late king,' the messenger announces. 'Yevonians have been instructed to wear black for three days. Would you like for the court to wear black as well, Your Majesty?'

Ragnar's lips form the word 'No', but I cut him off.

'Yes.'

'Very well, Ma'am.' As he leaves, there's a knock on the door. I jump.

'Enter!' A pair of medics creep into the room. Ragnar signals for them to speak.

'We are here to examine Her Majesty's injuries.'

'Come forth.'

The nurse breathes into my ear as the head medic examines my leg. I stand so they can examine my back, which is now packed with herbs. The ground is much further below me than I'm used to. I sway with my new height.

Ragnar bellows something. The assistant hops down a step. I bristle, rigid with the realisation that this woman was on the same level as me. Thankfully, when she goes to prod her stubby fingers in my face, the head medic waves her away. 'I will do that, thank you, Nurse.' The head medic, on the other hand, never goes past the second step, so she's never on the same level as a me. I like her.

'It is doing well, Your Majesty,' she tells me modestly as I sit back down, 'but I predict that you will have a little scarring.'

She places her tools in her bag and leaves, the young nurse hot on her heels.

*   *   *

There's not much to do sitting on a throne. It may be the most desirable chair in the world, but it's extremely uncomfortable. Ragnar takes the opportunity to exert his power over every trivial issue. I'm trapped in my own thoughts.

In a way, I respect him for taking the lengths he did to get here. I also despise him for it, of course. *Don't I?* I mourn Angus every day, but I can't shake off what Ragnar said; that it was my hand that killed— Oh, and I still haven't told Flossie!

'Jane?'

The lanky attendant by the wall darts her eyes to her hands, clasped neatly in front of her. 'Your Majesty?'

I'm still not sure about that title. 'Send a group of marshals to the cobblestone path leading from the castle to the forest.' I wince, and draw in a breath before continuing, 'There's a horse's body there, covered by a travelling cloak. Tell them to bring it here for burial.'

'Yes, Your Majesty.'

'That is all.' Ragnar dismisses her on my behalf. Paying a final respect, the attendant leaves the room.

FLOSSIE

NOW

I TRACE MY eyes over the bottles on the pantry shelf. Their labels are peeling, but I can just about make out the contents. I swear I saw a rat run across the shelf earlier.

I ache with homesickness, for both my old life and my new one. I spent so many happy summer days helping my father with his medicines in our hometown; for the whole rotation of the sun, my five sisters and I would tinker with his tools and trial our own remedies. By the time I was seven, I could recite every plant in our hometown and list its qualities. I came to the Clearing with a goal of helping people like he did, but I've made things worse for those I love. Have I failed him?

Cider's alone with Bramble, Basil's ruling beside a (*Mother of Nature, forgive my treason*) mass murderer because of me, and I never taught the girls how to jump their horses!

A key jangles in the door. I stop plaiting my hair.

'Are you decent?'

'Yes, come in!'

My chamber attendant pushes the door open with her foot, balancing a tray of bread and gruel over her palms. 'Your food, Miss.' She places the tray on the bed forced into the corner. I sit down next to it. The straw mattress sags and groans underneath me, tipping gruel onto her sleeve. I gasp and stand up. Cursing, she dabs at the stain frantically, but it's already soaked into the black fabric.

'Mother's macula, I'm so sorry!' I splutter. She flashes me a look and I well up a little.

'The king has requested your presence, Miss.'

My stomach turns to metal. The dank air in the badly lit chamber thickens. *Surely not more torture?*

'Thank you, I'll attend shortly. And sorry again for the stain.'

She exits without another word, leaving the door unlocked. The food curls its grey lips up at me. My plait falls apart in my sore hands, so I abandon it and head for the throne room. The king does not like to be kept waiting.

I place my fingers on the wall for stability and follow the spiral staircase down, the earthy scent of my chamber fading with each step. My hand traces the rippling wall until it reaches an alcove. I take a moment to look out of the grated window at the vast gardens. The view really boasts the extent of Mother's ability; past the gardens, forests the colour of flames stretch for suns. A strange brown blob has appeared on the cobblestone path, but it's too far away for me to make out. A hawk soaring across the orange sky draws my eyes up to the purple mountains lining the horizon. If I squint hard enough, I can see the dip in the trees below, where my village is. Longing pangs in my chest. I hurry down the rest of the stairs before sentiment gets the better of me.

'Enter!' The new king booms from inside the great hall. *Mother's metacarpals, why does he shout for everything?* The guards thrust open the door.

The royals loom over me, draped in fabulous fabrics. Basil's fine, dark robes hug her figure beautifully. And they're long, so long that they spill over the steps. Some girls would give anything to have a frame like hers. Little fly-always escape her elaborate plaits. Someone else must have done them for her, as she can't find her own parting yet. If we ever get out of this mess, I'll teach her. The king broods like the night sky next to her, sucking in her usual warmth. She's pale, drained, lifeless. I should never have let her go.

Sugar! I fix my eyes on the floor. The biggest unspoken rule of the castle is to, under no circumstances, look up at the royals.

'Why are you not wearing black?' the king demands. I rub the bumps on my arms through my canary-yellow cotton sleeves. I hate this fabric, and the colour, but at least it's lively. 'Black, Your Majesty?'

'The country is in mourning. Do you think you are so above everyone that you can disregard the direct orders of the monarchy? We've been courteous enough to provide you with garments, and this is how you repay us?'

My heart plummets. 'No, Sir…'

He sucks in a breath and purses his lips. I tuck my head in, preparing for the blast of cruel words to inevitably follow.

'Ragnar, stop!' Basil's mousy voice fills my ears instead. 'I've not told her yet!'

I picked at the cracked epidermis on my hands. Told me what? I file through my memory, frantically searching for anything I might have missed. I would never dare to displease the king deliberately. Whenever I do, Basil always faces the consequences instead. I should have told her that the king had sent for me before she left.

The king grunts. 'Go on then, my angel, tell her.'

I chance a look up at Basil. She has her fingers to her mouth, swallowing hard.

'Come on, Bas, out with it!'

I snap my eyes back down.

'We aren't actually mourning Vesuvius. We need the public to believe that.' She won't meet my eye. 'We are mourning because… Angus is dead.' She mumbles the last three words, as if she doesn't believe them yet.

'Okay…' I hope my face is calm for her sake because my stomach is reeling from the blow. 'How did he die?'

'He was stabbed,' I made out through her muffling hand. My heart leaps into my mouth.

'By whom?' I desperately want to run forwards and hug her. How could anyone do such a thing to Basil?

She's so sweet! *I'll find whoever did it and sort them out.* 'Bas— Your Majesty, who did this to you?'

'I did.'

Oh no, sweetheart. No, no, no. That's awful. The guilt she must feel! She loved Angus dearly.

Before I can say another word, the king fires off the information about the funeral. Then he waves his hand, and I'm escorted back to my chamber.

I sit on the hard bed, staring at the gruel. It's so selfish of me to be upset about Angus's death when Basil is the one who is suffering the most. But I will burst if I hold these tears back any longer. Maybe I'm being too harsh on myself; Basil does have a tiny part in this whole thing. She should have listened to me.

No! Mother, forgive me for my treasonous thoughts!

But are they treasonous? No one had an issue spitting treasonous insults about the late King Vesuvius. Cider always complained that I never put my own emotions first. Father always taught me that mental health was just as important as physical health. My heart aches for Angus. My heart aches for Bramble and Cider. My heart aches for my old life. I miss them so much. What's wrong with that? It only shows the Mother that I love them unconditionally.

On that note, a sob breaks the dam behind my eyes, and I cry to soothe my aching heart.

BASIL

NOW

WARM, PLEASANT SUNLIGHT splashes my face. The soft chattering of birds outside fills my chamber. The castle is alive with early morning activity. I settle back down into the pillows, smiling.

Oh. This is not a dream; this is reality, and I hate it. The air snakes under the fur, icy and thin. The curtains around the four-poster bed press in around me, so I force myself to get up. I free myself quickly and dip behind my dressing screen, the air nipping at my ankles.

A cry rips from my throat at my wedding garment: the tailors have just bleached my funeral dress to make it white. Ragnar could have done better than that. I get that all of this was very sudden, but as the queen I expected a new dress. I'll confront him later, but for now, well, what choice do I have?

Flossie, my maid of honour, raps on the door. I dust off my nightwear and call her in. She's lucky to be attending; it took everything I had to convince Ragnar that she wouldn't cause any trouble. 'Good morning, Your Majesty.' She brandishes a comb in one hand and a bundle of long- stemmed gerberas in the other.

'Flossie, how many times?' I plop myself on the floor. 'It's Basil to you.' It's the least I can offer her to repay for her torture.

'Your leg seems better,' Flossie says, as she sits on my bed and begins parting my hair. I can never manage to do it myself. The occasional scuttle of her fingers working their magic breaks up the dead air as she twists the flowers into my plaits.

She jerks her hand away from my head suddenly, wincing in pain.

'What is it?'

My friend nurses her calloused hand. 'Just sore.' I grab a glass bowl from my dressing table and remove the lid. She scoops out a little of the gel and rubs it in. I replace the lid clumsily and put the bowl down with a chink. She sighs with the immediate relief the gel provides. 'Thank you. I didn't know they had aloe vera here!' *So that's what that is!*

'No problem. The medic gave it to me for my injuries…' Grief crushes my chest as Flossie helps me into my dress and laces it up. Once it's on, she flits around me with a small fabric blade, adjusting it with a slice here, a chop there, until I'm wearing a completely different dress. She stands behind me and wraps a lacy outer corset around my body. My chest squeezes. The pop of green makes me sting with despair again. Flossie's face drops as she remembers the colour of Angus's ribbon too.

A mosaic of scents waft in from the kitchen. 'That smells nice,' she comments, easing the heavy silence.

'Extremely,' I reply. I would love for her famous apple pie to be at the banquet instead.

She pins my cloak together and adjusts it, so it frames my shoulders. Admiring her handiwork in the polished silver mirror, I lower the circlet onto my head, careful not to tug at my plaits. Power washes through me. The outfit is beautiful.

Whilst Flossie dabs makeup on my scars, I peer at myself in the mirror over her shoulder. 'Augh!' I cry in disgust; there's a huge, bulging spot disrupting my freckles.

'What is it?' Flossie exclaims, 'Did I hurt you?' She sees the ugly spot. 'Ah. Don't worry, Basil, I'll fix it.' Concentration riddles her blotchy face as she smothers the spot furiously with powder. I forgot about her acne. She must have covered it extremely well to pass the examinations. Perhaps I shouldn't have made such a fuss, but a queen needs to look perfect on her wedding day.

'Oh, Floss, it's just so hard!' I wail.

'Yes, sweetheart,' she says dryly. As if she knows anything about suffering.

'You're happily married.' I snap, 'What do you know about pain?'

She mutters something under her breath. Fury rolls through me. How dare she argue with the queen? As awful as the circumstances are, this is still my special day. What makes her think she can steal the attention?

'I don't think this is the time for backchat, being as it was your husband's sword that killed Angus!' I growl at her.

She stops fussing with my makeup and stares at me with furious hazel eyes. 'And who was holding the sword?' she retorts. 'Basil, can't you see? Angus's death was an accident, but this whole thing is partly your fault. And don't drag Cider into this. You only needed that sword because I took Ragnar's daggers away to protect you. And every time I tried to tell you the king had sent for me, you shot me down!'

So, she stole from me as well? 'That's 'Your Majesty' to you! And I've always listened to what you have to say!' Even as I say it, I'm lying, but I'm not backing down yet. 'Alright, maybe I haven't, but you should have tried harder!'

'Tried harder?' She winces at her treasonous outburst, but it doesn't deter her. 'It's impossible to make you listen! And I'm sick of you putting me in the shadows!'

'Well, if you think that way, why are you still here?'

'To get you ready for the fated wedding you got yourself into! It's not like I could leave anyway!'

'Ssh, stop shouting!'

She lowers her voice a fraction. 'Listen, Your Majesty, for once in your life. I can forgive you for my torture and Angus's death, but if you marry the king, we'll be no better off than before!'

How stupid is she? 'And how can I say no? Do you want more torture?'

'I don't care! He can gouge out my eyes and parade me round the Clearing by my hair, but I won't stand for you marrying him. Not after what he's done to you! If you don't listen to me now, he'll worm his way further into your head. And if he can kill forty-eight people then he won't hesitate to kill more. Basil, 'twill never end! He's an awful man and an unfit ruler!'

'That's enough!' I bang my fist on the vanity. 'Don't talk about Ragnar like that! He murdered them for me!'

'Basil, tell me you'll say no. You can't give in again. Let him kill me, but whatever you do, do not agree to marry him.'

'Flossie, if you carry on shouting, you'll alert the guards, and Ragnar will lock you straight back up again! I suggest you get out for your own sake.'

Defeated, Florencia scrunches her nose. 'Fine. Don't listen to me. You can see how far that's got you.'

As she leaves, I can't help myself. 'See how far that's got you,' I mimic, as the door closes behind her.

I turn to examine the girl in the mirror. She releases a pent-up breath and adjusts her crown; it slipped when she flew into a rage. She simmers with anger, like a delicate candle flame. But other than that…

RAGNAR

NOW

SHE IS STUNNING. It takes everything I have to keep my jaw off the floor as my angel glides down the aisle. Her jasmine dress trails behind her like wings. Her presence alone makes the doves on the ceremonial drapes fly from their woven confines. Sunlight kisses her cheeks and strokes the freckles speckled across her nose, illuminating them like the night sky has lent its stars to her. Even the Mother of Nature bows before her beauty. She steps delicately, like a doe, careful not to disturb the ground beneath her. Bas hands her bundle of flowers off to Florencia, who snatches them angrily. I don't want her here, but my fiancée does and if it makes her happy, I'll welcome it.

I take her ring from the cushion. It is excellently crafted and adorned with a sapphire to match her large, enchanting eyes—only the finest for my queen.

She's in front of me, the scent of fresh flowers radiating from her hair. My wedding makeup feels cakey in comparison to her light complexion. The head elder hobbles forwards, tainting her scent with his mustiness, and begins to read. 'Due to the secrecy of the wedding, there are no public objections to joining this pair in matrimony. Are there any reasons from the court as to why this pair should not be united in the eyes of the Father of Fate or the Mother of Nature? Speak now or forever hold your peace.'

Silence. Such a beautiful sound.

'Splendid, we'll begin. Do you, Your Majesty Queen Basilia Eldnic' – he gestures at my beautiful lady – 'take His Majesty King Ragnar Vernentide to be your lawfully wedded husband?'

Hesitation plays in her eyes. 'Say it, Bas,' I urge. Florencia fidgets in the crowd. Basil follows my gaze. Her lip quivers. *No, face me, my sublime lady, and let me look at you.* She reads my mind, and I gasp, drowning in her splendour once again. She picks at the fabric on her gorgeous dress.

'Ragnar,' she breathes. My name is golden in her mouth. I bask in its glory, in its power. If there's one thing I can thank Vesuvius for, it's this moment. This marriage makes it all worth it.

'I don't think I can.' Her glow drops. Clearly, I've misheard. 'What?'

'You heard me, Ragnar, I've reconsidered…'

I laugh nervously. *She can't do this to me.*

'Very funny, eh, Bas?' I give her a playful thump on the arm. She shies away.

'No, Ragnar, I'm not joking. I can't do this.'

My blue blood races under my skin. My hopes, my dreams, my perception of love all shatter. I must stay calm and handle this in a civilised manner.

BASIL

NOW

'THIS WAS SUPPOSED to be perfect!' Ragnar howls, stomping his feet. 'I killed all those people for this day!' He runs to the display on the wall and pulls at a sword. It refuses to budge as it's nailed to the wall. 'Get me a sword!' he roars, spraying droplets of spittle through the air. I've never seen people move so fast; no one wants to be the last out of the room.

'No!' Ragnar spits at Flossie as she edges towards the door. 'You stay here.'

Ragnar doesn't do anything to restrain us, but his crazed stare traps me where I stand. The servants return, all empty-handed and sheepish, except for one; Caspar, the unlucky bearer, holds out the sword proudly, but his hands are shaking. I always liked Caspar. It's a shame that he's the person handing Ragnar the sword. Neither man will meet my eye.

Ragnar snatches the sword and drives through the gaggle of lingering servants towards—*no!*—Flossie. He grabs her by the hair, forces her onto her knees and puts the sword to her throat, sending my stomach spiralling.

'Ragnar, stop!' I plead.

'I just want you to be happy!' White-hot tears burn into his red face. Flossie, on the other hand, is so pale my dress looks almost pink in contrast.

'Ragnar, this isn't what I want!' I try to approach him, but malice twists his face. I step back.

'Then what do you want?' His eyebrows knit together. 'What am I doing wrong? Tell me, Bas, because I want to give you what you want as soon as possible!'

'I want you to let Flossie go and give up this delusion! I was happier before all this. Yes, I wanted Vesuvius dead, but I didn't want to take his place! I don't want the burden of the throne! It's too much.' I long to drag Flossie from his arms, but he'd rip her throat open. 'Elizabeth, please, stop him!'

The attendant shakes her head at me mournfully. 'No can do, Your Majesty. The king's orders take priority.'

I'm going to be sick.

'You! Fetch me another sword,' Ragnar commands Elizabeth, his voice cracking. The room sways. Ragnar's going to kill me, and he's going to make Flossie watch. Elizabeth bows her head and leaves.

Oh, Mother help me. The sword Elizabeth returns with is the one Cider gave me. She kneels before Ragnar, extending the blade over her palms. But Ragnar refuses it.

'Not for me.' He inhales shakily and points with the tip of his weapon. 'Her.' He's pointing it at me. What desperate game is he playing now? Elizabeth gets up, moves over to me and repeats the action. With trembling fingers, I take the cumbersome sword in my hand. *I killed Angus with this.* The blade sheens red in the light. My throat clamps shut.

'Now leave us alone.' The crowd murmurs with relief, and we're left alone.

'Basil.' Ragnar's voice is quiet and deadly. He's stopped crying. 'Listen to me carefully: kill me and she lives. Kill her and we can talk this through.'

He's making me prove who I love the most. That hopelessly romantic son of a bitch.

RAGNAR

NOW

I TUG ON FLORENCIA's tangled hair, her curls loop-ing around my fingers, and touch my sword to her neck. She squirms beneath my weapon. I don't care. She's stolen Basil from me, and I'll kill her if I must. This worked once, it'll work again. I press the icy blade into her skin, welling up tiny jewels of blood beneath it. She cries out in pain. I would much prefer to use my dag-gers, but you can't be fussy with spur-of-the-moment threatening tactics.

'So, what's it going to be, Bas?' I press the blade further with each word. 'Your lifelong lover or your little—'

'Agh!'

'Blonde—'

'Basil!'

'Friend?'

BASIL

NOW

I SAVED YEVONIA from war!' Ragnar yells, 'Vesuvius, he didn't bring us over here just to populate; he bought us here to birth an unstoppable army! Make the right choice, Basil. Kill her. KILL HER! What can she give you? I'll get you whatever you want! Land? Done! Jewellery? Done! Screw it, if you want to send everyone in Yevonia home, I'll do it if only it will make you happy.'

Guilt overwhelms my throat. I fight to swallow it down. 'No, Ragnar! I don't want it!'

Oh, but I do.

This is Flossie's fault. She told me not to marry him and look where that's got us. Ragnar's right. What can Flossie give me that he can't? He's shed blood, so, so much blood—but for me. He's shed so much blood that he's become numb to anything else. But he did it so I can have jewels and fame and power— gold-encrusted clothing, the lavish queen life, my name forever woven into history.

I could replace the tapestry in the entrance hall. I can see it now: the Yevonians fall to their knees in thanks as I send them home. Florencia can't give me that honour. She'll never love me that much.

She told me this morning that she didn't mind if Ragnar killed her. I don't think I do either.

'If you aren't going to kill her, kill me! I'm a murderer!' Ragnar wails.

'But you did it to earn my love,' I murmur, turning the sword over on my palm.

His empty eyes brighten. 'Yes, I did, Bas. I will do anything if it is to make you smile!'

And scarily enough, I believe him.

Flossie stares me dead in the eye. If I let them both live, Ragnar will probably kill her anyway. Why wait? I'm sure she'll understand that she's a minor sacrifice.

FLOSSIE

NOW

BASIL ADJUSTS HER grip on her sword. She's chosen her path: forced happiness. We both draw in a breath. She raises her sword. She lunges.

I don't fight her. I just close my eyes and brace for impact. There's no more pressure on my neck, no fingers in my hair. Ragnar holds me at arm's length so Basil has a better aim. He's still talking. I wish he'd be quiet so I can ascend to the Mother of Nature and her partner in peace. They are letting this happen for reasons I may never know, but if it's what they see as right then it must be so.

Cider is strong. He'll get through this. He has Domino to keep him company and my parents won't know any different.

My heart drums desperately for the last time, as if to make up for all the seasons it's about to lose. I inhale Basil's flowery aroma deeply, the scent getting stronger as she darts forwards. Finally, the detached sound of a sword plunging into flesh fills the room, followed by a strangled gulp of air.

Tranquillity.

Too much tranquillity. There is no searing, icy pain; Death's cold fingers can't have taken me yet, I'm sure of it. I open my eyes. The hilt of Basil's sword protrudes from a heaving chest. But it's not mine.

Ragnar, eyes wide in shock, hunches over the sword in his abdomen. His mouth is frozen, still forming his speech as he slumps against the wall. *Mother's meninges, that's a lot of blood.* His crown slips from his head, and the sound of the metal slicing against the gold floor echoes around the throne room.

RAGNAR

NOW

I AM DYING in Basil's arms. Tears encrust her majestic lashes and run down her cheeks in sparkling water-falls. I cry out, but phlegm fills my throat. How long will it be until we reunite again?

My whole body is tense around the blade, but it doesn't hurt. This must be right if this is what she wants. Or maybe she missed her target. Well, she was always a clumsy dancer.

See you at the end of the world, my stunning little angel.

BASIL

NOW

Ragnar smiles at me, sadly. His once strikingly green eyes are glassy. A tear trickles down his cheek. Blood trails from his mouth. I take him in my arms. His body is warm. Wispy breaths snake from his parted lips. 'It's for the best,' I promise him, but I'm trying to convince myself as much as anything. He's done everything in his power for me, but Flossie always listened. She is my true happiness and it's time I returned the favour. The king has been overthrown.

*   *   *

He's trying to say something. I release him. He spits out a mouthful of blood, and I wipe his mouth with my sleeve. His voice is wispy, but I can about make his words out before they die on his lips. 'Are you happy, Basil?' he gurgles through the blood.

I don't know. Am I?

'I'm not…' I need more time. I can't make this decision now.

His head hangs, and he slumps forwards. My arm naturally unhooks from his bulky shoulders. I push his head up gently to look at his face.

His open eyes have faded out. The steady rise and fall of his chest has stopped. There's a familiar look about him. It was in Angus's eyes before I covered his body. It's Death, smiling at me from his soul.

I plant a kiss on his balmy lips. But I'm kissing his corpse. It's too late to answer his last question, but I do it anyway.

'No. I'm not happy. I want you back. I want you back. I can't live with this. Come back, please, Ragnar. Ragnar!'

I curl up into a screaming ball. I did this. I hate myself. I killed Angus, I killed Ragnar. The walls are caving in around us, smoke smothers everything. Spiralling wisps of rubble fill every fibre of my being. I have two minds. I am not me. Ragnar. Dead. Again. By this hand. Angus. I'm falling, breaking, drowning. Basil. What does that word mean? I don't know anymore, I don't know anything…

Basil. It's vaguely familiar. Basil. Basil. It's a soothing word.

FLOSSIE

NOW

‘Basil!’ she can't hear me. She's lying on the floor, her hands pressed over her ears and her eyes squeezed shut. My best friend mutters nonsense. It's terrifying. Forgetting all my father's training, I run over and smack her. Hard. It doesn't register, so I do it again.

Eventually, she comes round. *Thank the Mother.* She looks at me, lost. I grab her and pull her to my chest. She sobs and sobs, staining my dress with blood and tears, but I don't care. I'm so glad I've not lost her to her own mind. 'It's okay, Basil, I'm here, sweetheart,' I croon into her hair. We rock together until the sobbing becomes pained whimpering, and finally, she sleeps.

BASIL

SIXTY SEASONS LATER

Shadows seep from the trees, clawing towards me, nipping at my horse's ankles. I don't want to do this.

Will Confederation's Clearing (formally Magnate's Clearing) have changed more than just its name since I last saw it? I've held off visiting since my coronation, but it's about time I got over my grief. Besides, the only way to overcome something is to march into it, head held high.

Despite my attempt at a positive mindset, I'm not much like the brave queen I'm supposed to be as we enter the woods. My legs shake uncontrollably, confusing my horse. My accompanying guards roll their eyes behind my back. I hold my nerve long enough to get the beautiful black stallion past the first tree and I pat his glossy coat. This horse doesn't replace Angus, but he keeps me company.

Angus's memorial still stands, but age browns his

facial lines and moss sprouts from his ears. Domino also grows old, for now her grey hair is wiry and her bones clack when she walks. Flossie perches carefully on her back for the last time before her horse's retirement.

The wind howls in my ears; it howls his name. *This is not real.* I shut my eyes and wrangle with my laboured breaths. The forest comes back into clarity. Domino's bones creak as she plods behind us.

Alastair looks back at Flossie. 'Mother, what's it like?'

'What's what like, sweetheart?' she asks him.

Alastair, Flossie's son, is my heir, as I don't have any children myself to bear the burden of the throne when I'm gone. Unlike me, he's been raised in the castle to prepare him for kingship. It's about time he visits the Clearing he will one day oversee. 'Your old village. Whenever I bring it up, you always say "I'll tell you when you're older," but I'm sure that's just parent code for "I'm going to hope you forget so I don't have to tell you."'

Flossie flushes. 'Cider, why don't you tell him?'

Cider chuckles at her pleading face. 'I'll let you answer that one, Flo. He can handle it, big strong lad like him.'

'Well,' she exhales deeply, ''twas a different place when I went to get your father all those seasons ago. Very dull, coaly, but everyone was relieved. Everywhere you looked people were dressed in black to mourn King Vesu—'

Alastair cuts her off, 'No, I meant before Aunty Basilia's coronation!'

Flossie gives me a small smile and relaxes in her saddle. Talking about the Clearing in mourning always makes her twitchy. Especially the bit when Cider found out about her torture.

'Aunty Basilia' was Alastair's fond title for me, courtesy of Flossie's suggestion that we were 'almost like sisters'.

'Well, we mainly had good times, but we couldn't really enjoy them because King Vesuvius did some awful things to us. Saying people hated him is probably an understatement…'

My horse slips. I tense, gripping the rein with white knuckles. He regains his balance, but my muscles stay knotted with nerves.

Hooves clip on dry bark as we talk the journey away. 'Oh, it doesn't half hurt riding side-saddle,' I moan.

'I know, right?' Cider jokes.

Alastair chimes in, 'But Father, you're riding astride.'

'I'm just messing with her, Alastair.' Cider leans over and bops him on the nose. Needle-like tears prick my eyes. I pick at a loose thread on my glove, choking back a sob. Flossie stops laughing and gives me a questioning thumbs up. Mother bless her, she was always so observant.

'Hey.' Cider prods me with his covered sword. 'You good?'

I needed to kill Angus, or he would have killed me. It doesn't mean I don't love him, nor that I don't mourn him. It only means that it's now my duty to spread the respect for his and Ragnar's loyalty by educating the public of the noble actions they took for me.

I return the gesture to Flossie, answering Cider with, 'Yes, thanks.'

Gradually, the trees thin out, and the air swells with boiling fruit, sugary and warm. We are home.

NOW

I BREATHE IN the sunlight as it splays through the saplings. It's so good to be back. The outline of a colourful crowd grows and thrives, the people shoving to get a glimpse of their queen. Our messenger blares his trumpet, and the horses come to a halt as the gathering bursts into applause.

Is it wrong that my subjects are applauding me for murder? *These same subjects loathed Vesuvius for the same thing.* This is quite different though. Because of the sacrifices made by everyone I love, the Yevonians know they are free. Then who deserves this applause? *The king is dead, but by whose hand?* Ragnar killed King Vesuvius, but I killed King Ragnar.

I guess only the Father knows.

These questions swirl in my mind as we ride down the main path. Wafts of spices and berries weave through the streets, dodging the rustle of hurried footsteps. I smile and wave politely at my community. A few unfamiliar faces stick out in the crowd; however, the parents either side of them are old friends. A sizzling pig turns on a spit outside the butcher's. My stomach growls. Hands reach out and fingertips graze my boots. Manure lingers in the air, but there's none on this street. Spending sixty seasons in a pristine castle has made my nose more sensitive than usual.

There's a sweaty press of bodies. My horse raises his silky head and snorts. What if he kicks out? People lean out from the open windows of the jutting, half-timbered houses to sprinkle us with food and flowers. My lungs harden at the overstimulation. I need to get out of this crushing crowd. I look at Flossie, and she signals to a guard. He holds up his palm, halting the procession, and a hush falls over the village.

'Step back from Her Majesty!' he booms across the street.

There is a hum of annoyed muttering as the crowd shuffles back an inch or two. At least I can breathe again.

'Basil?' Flossie calls over the crowd's grumbles.

'One sec—' *No, Basil, listen to what she has to say.* 'Yes, Flossie?'

'Can we get some cooking apples whilst we're here?'

I shrug. 'Who here sells cooking apples?' I ask the crowd. The Yevonians exchange confused glances; why does the queen want apples? But they part to reveal an elderly woman, shaking with the effort of raising her bony arm. Flossie lets out a small squeak of joy. 'Lead the way,' I command as the woman makes a respectable attempt at a curtsey.

She drags her way down the street, our horses tripping over their own hooves as they try to keep in time with her slow pace.

Folk swarm us again, but a stern look from the

guard and a quick flash of sword makes them back off. We reach her house and she pushes open the door. It screams on its hinges as a herb-laced dust cloud bursts from the frame. We dismount, and hand our horses off to the guards. The lady potters up to Flossie.

'Lady Florence, isn't it?' she croaks.

'Florencia,' she corrects. 'Well, call me Flossie. Mother's midfoot, I've not seen you in seasons! How are you, sweetheart?'

'Still marching on. Who's this little critter?' She pinches Alastair's cheek, much to his disgust.

'This is Alastair Eric Rose, my son.'

'And my heir,' I add.

She bows her head. 'Your Highness.'

How does Flossie know this woman? Upon closer inspection of the lady's face, I gasp: *it's the Wise Woman who tried to relieve me of my grief!* The weathered skin droops from her face and her bones are brittle, but the shadow of a smile dances in her eyes. She recognises me too.

Like her, the house is clinging on to its structure for dear life. Dust coats every surface, so much so that the Wise Woman seems to have a layer of dust herself. She lights a hazy candle and descends into her pantry, the bones in her knees grinding together all the way down.

Why does Flossie need these specific apples? We have perfectly good apples in the castle gardens. I raise a questioning eyebrow at her. She winks back. *Flossie… apples… Yevonia…* I've got it! My heart floods with sunshine; she's going to make an apple pie!

The Wise Woman trudges back up the stairs. Her parchment-thin knuckles grip a basket full of cooking apples. She shoves it into a guard's chest, who takes it, flustered, and tips the contents into his travelling sack. I grin at her and open my purse to pay. 'How much?'

She stares at her dirty floor, her thin lips forming the words, 'Nothing, Your Majesty.'

Oh, for the Mother's sake. It takes every ounce of my dignity not to roll my eyes at yet another person treating me differently because I wear a ring of metal on my head and sit on a fancy chair. 'How much are they normally?'

'Nothing, Your Majesty.'

I grit my teeth. She's stubborn, but not as stubborn as me. 'As Queen of Yevonia, I demand you tell me—' I stop as the Wise Woman pulls a sign from the crate and turns it round so I can see. It reads:

'Cooking apples, free. Help yourself.'

My stomach drops. I splutter an apology and she blinks her forgiveness at me.

The guard rifles through the apples. He bites into one, to check it for poison, but spits it out immediately. Cooking apples are more bitter than he thought.

'Take care!' I call to her. We shut the door on the quiet of her slightly stale house, and re-enter the blinding hubbub outside.

*   *   *

I'm not ready to go back to my old house. I'm not ready to see my wedding cloak or Ragnar's notes. I'm not ready to see the rooms where we used to dance. I'm not ready to see its empty stables or the rusting cutlery left on the side. At least mould won't have taken over; Flossie threw all the uneaten food away for me. (Yet another thing she's done that I'll be eternally grateful for.) But before my speech there's one more thing she and I want to do.

*   *   *

Alastair picks at the grass in the meadow. The river looks enticing, but we don't feel like paddling. The barley rippling in the breeze tickles my arms. I shiver, despite the heat, and wrap my arms tightly around my violet dress, now void of the gold stitches. The colour no longer symbolises superiority, but rather unity and justice for the long-suffering Yevonians. Flossie dons her signature pink overcoat on a cream dress and we plaited our own hair to compliment each other's.

We watch from the bank as Domino paces the meadow, almost like she can smell him. I ache for her loss. Whilst the ache has not gotten any better, every day Angus's death haunts me less and less.

DOMINO

NOW

His presence is with me. Soon, I can join him amongst the stars. I don't mind leaving Flossie and Basil behind. They will join us later.

With a gust of wind, he's here. His ghostly figure watches me from across the meadow. I whinny with delight and run towards him. He swishes his mane, mischief sparkling in his eyes. I kick out and fart with excitement, trotting around him in a circle, inviting him to follow me.

And together we run, until our chests burn and our legs scream. With the natural spirit flowing through our bodies, we tumble over each other, lost in our make-believe land. For a moment, the stiffness in my legs disappears. We lap the meadow again, and he leaps over me. I flip my head to see where he is…

But he's gone. I'm left alone in the meadow, the wind whistling his goodbye.

FLOSSIE

NOW

WE TAKE OUR seats upon the makeshift stage. There are so many eyes on me. I bob my knee as heat paints my face. Basil takes my hand and squeezes it gently. I smile softly, warmth spreading through my chest as the messenger announces the reason for our visit..

BASIL

NOW

FLOSSIE BEAMS DOWN at our joined hands. The air buzzes with chatter around us. Children, men and women of all ages stare up at us with awe. One face … is that? It can't be. Her features are too sharp, and her long grey hair is fluffy. No, I'm right; it is Beatriz! And that's Julian, Wren and Bronwyn standing behind her! Oh, how I want to run down the stairs and hug them! They all look amazing!

I zone back in to catch the tail end of my name; my cue. There will be plenty of time to catch up in seasons to come. I stand on my wobbly legs and make my way over to the podium. The messenger places a pre-written speech in the centre of the stand. The words swim on the page. Oh, please help me, Mother of Nature, I'm such a mess of a sovereign. The words come into focus, but they are dry and emotionless. I ignore the script, open my mouth and let the words stream out.

'I would like to start by informing you that, as of today, transport vessels to and from Yevonia are no longer forbidden. You are free to reunite with your families.'

The crowd explodes with joy.

When the cheers die down, I continue. 'And as queen, it is my duty to credit the sacrifices that have led to this jubilant moment.

'First of all, thank you to the Father of Fate. He may have broken me down, but he did it so I could build myself up to where I am now. Also, the Mother of Nature for the blessing of those who love me.' I smile at Flossie. 'Next, I must thank Lady Florencia Rose. Because of her brave actions, this island is no longer on its knees, under the rule of another tyrant. My days of ignoring her judgement are over.'

She flushes with pride. Someone claps, triggering a true Yevonian-style, rapturous applause. All for her. And, by the Mother and Father, she deserves every minute of it.

'Now, I must admit, I have not been entirely truthful,' I continue. 'You see, King Vesuvius did not die of old age, he was murdered.' As expected, murmurs break out. I wait for silence.

'When I came over to Yevonia, I met a man who would do anything to make me happy. He was gracious, funny and made the best stew. He risked his own life for me. But he lied. He threatened his best friend's family. He murdered. He murdered a lot. His name was King Ragnar Vernentide, and it was he who killed King Vesuvius.'

A river of emotions filter through the faces as I

unearth my story. Making this public is a huge risk, not to mention I'm a female monarch, but I don't fear Death; I'm too familiar with her. She's a stinging, backstabbing bitch who kicks you when you're down. She snakes into everyone's life eventually, contorting it beyond recognition. Yet if you crave nothing more than her mercy, she slithers from your grasp. But when the dust settles, it's her cruelty that makes you stronger. We're taught from an early age that hardship breeds stamina. She gives it as both our greatest enemy and our greatest weapon. And for that, she is one of the Mother's greatest creations. Some may even say she's an angel.

A scuffle breaks out as a handful of people realise that I'm somewhat responsible for unnecessary executions. Guards escort the thrashing revenge-seekers away. Others just stand there and loathe silently.

'I can't bring your families back, but I hope it helps, even a tiny bit, knowing that the king died feeling as betrayed as you do.' My voice breaks with pity and my palms glisten with sweat. 'After all his efforts, it was the woman he tried to give the world to who drove her sword through his chest. If that's not betrayal, I don't know what is.'

I sip the water on the stand and try to gather my thoughts.

'Me,' I clarify. 'I killed King Ragnar.'

Acid tinges in my throat. A scribe scribbles my words down furiously, inking them into history.

'He was a merciless dictator, but if King Ragnar was

anything, it wasn't selfish. I do genuinely believe that he did it all for my happiness. His last words were not wasted by telling me what to do with his riches or asking me to make him famous for saving your children from war. No, his last words were, 'Are you happy, Basil?' But he died before I could reply. And if that's not true devotion, I don't know what is.'

I exhale. What I put myself through was extremely unfair, but telling my people has cleared my head.

'Are you?' a voice from the crowd cuts through the pulsing hush. I skim my eyes over the shocked faces, but I can't find the speaker.

'Am I what?'

'Apologies, Your Majesty, for being so abrupt.' A young man shoves his way to the front. 'What I meant was, are you happy?'

I swallow. I've tossed this question over and over in my mind every sleepless night since Ragnar died. The Clearing is clearly happy; the people's once sunken, dull faces now shine with hope. Flossie beams at me, the raw marks on her back evident of her days of torture. Alastair smiles up at his mother as Cider squeezes his wife's shoulder lovingly. I'm not quite at peace with myself for murdering Ragnar. I'm not quite at peace with myself for stabbing Angus. I'm not quite at peace with myself for Flossie's torture. But I'll get there eventually.

So, am I happy?

I turn back to face my people.

'Yes,' I decide. 'Yes, I am.'

ACKNOWLEDGEMENTS

Where do I even start? How can I ever begin to thank the people that made my biggest dream come true? As cheesy as it sounds, twelve-year-old me would scream with delight if she knew that we made it: we published a book!

But I couldn't have done it alone; behind every good book is an army of supporters, and here are mine: thank you, Mum, for bringing me into the world and constantly going above and beyond for me and this project. Thank you, Dad, for not only reading this far into a book but also engaging in my endless *Castlebound*-related rants. And how could I forget, your contribution of my author photo! Thanks Tom, my brother, for your enthusiasm and King Vesuvius's name. Thank you to my school librarian, Mrs Palfreyman, for your constant encouragement and reading the early drafts! (I am truly sorry about what I did to Angus!) Also thank you to all the teachers who have supported my writing throughout the years.

Thank you so much to the team at White Magic Publishing Studios, without them you would not be holding this book in your hands now. An especially big thank you to Lynne Walker, my amazing editor, whose selflessness and empathy should inspire future generations. Thank you to Francesca Cosanti for creating my *stunning* book cover and giving life to the words. Thank you Gareth Collinson for your patient proofreading and formatting, for which I will be eternally grateful. Thank you Dinah Drazin for the beautiful typesetting, you captured my vision perfectly!

Thank you, Milan Tutt and Auntie Caroline, for letting me use your computers when my own device was acting up. I couldn't have done it without you both! Milan, I wish you all the best in the future as you absolutely deserve it. Caroline, stay as awesome as you are already! Thank you, George Greaves, for your invaluable suggestions when BETA reading and your undying enthusiasm throughout. And to the amazing author, Abbie Emmons, your videos made this whole process a million times easier!

Thank you to all the family and friends not mentioned here who have been with *Castlebound* from the beginning. And most of all, thank you to you for reading my book. You make this all worth it, and the fact that you have read this makes me lost for words. (which isn't very good if you're an author!) By engaging in *Castlebound*, you have made my characters come to life in so many ways, but, more importantly, you are the reason I wrote the original draft in the first place.

Keep on reading!

~Jess

ABOUT THE AUTHOR

JESS WHITAKER began writing *Castlebound* during national teacher strikes in 2023, aged just fourteen, and published it two years later. She lives and writes in Chesterfield, U.K. She enjoys painting, writing in autumn (armed with a latte) and hopes to self-publish again in the future, once she finishes school.

Castlebound is her debut novella.